"Get Off M[...] Snapped. "I [...] With Your Sh[...] I Don't Have To Put Up With You!"

"That's where you're wrong, sweetheart. Grazing rights give me access to my animals any damn time I want."

"I despise you!"

"Now that sounds just like a female," Sloan said coolly. "When does the name-calling start?"

Maggie shrieked with blind rage, and her hand leaped up, aiming for his insolent face. She'd never struck a man before, never even had the *urge* to strike a man before, but she wanted to wipe that smirk off his face so badly she ached.

Sloan caught her wrist an instant before her hand made contact with his cheek. When she came at him again, hissing and spitting like a little wildcat, he locked his arms around her. "Just remember who started this," he muttered.

What came next wasn't planned. She was up against him, breathing hard, and she smelled like a woman. And he just stopped thinking and kissed her.

Dear Reader:

Welcome to Silhouette Desire—sensual, compelling, believable love stories written by and for today's woman. When you open the pages of a Silhouette Desire, you open yourself up to a whole new world— a world of promising passion and endless love.

Each and every Silhouette Desire is a wonderful love story that is both sensuous *and* emotional. You're with the hero and heroine each and every step of the way—from their first meeting, to their first kiss . . . to their happy ending. You'll experience all the deep joys—and occasional tribulations—of falling in love.

In future months, look for Silhouette Desire novels from some of your favorite authors, such as Naomi Horton, Nancy Martin, Linda Lael Miller and Lass Small, just to name a few.

So go wild with Desire. You'll be glad you did!

Lucia Macro
Senior Editor

JACKIE
MERRITT

MAGGIE'S MAN

SILHOUETTE *Desire*

Published by Silhouette Books New York

America's Publisher of Contemporary Romance

SILHOUETTE BOOKS
300 East 42nd St., New York, N.Y. 10017

ISBN: 0-373-05587-0

First Silhouette Books printing August 1990

Printed in the U.S.A.

JACKIE MERRITT

and her husband live just outside of Las Vegas, Nevada. An accountant for many years, Jackie has happily traded numbers for words. Next to family, books are her greatest joy, both for reading and writing.

One

Coming home at the beginning of summer each year was always a special event for Maggie Holloway. "Home" was the Holloway cattle ranch, and it was situated in the lower part of Montana, only a few miles north of the Wyoming border. Maggie spent summers on the ranch and the rest of the year in Bozeman, where she taught English literature at the university. As Professor Holloway she was a respected part of the academic community in Bozeman, but it was plain Maggie Holloway who lightheartedly drove the two hundred miles back to the family ranch each June.

This year her parents, Bert and Sarah, weren't going to be there to greet her. They had passed through Bozeman several weeks before, and Bert had been flying high, happily immersed in his campaign for state senator. "Don't worry about the ranch," Bert had proclaimed. "Les Scoggins is still there and keeping an eye on the place."

"And taking good care of Rebel, I hope," Maggie had interjected. Rebel, a beautiful honey-colored Thoroughbred stallion, was her pride and joy, and another reason why she started getting antsy the minute the winter weather broke each year. She enjoyed teaching, but she would be less than honest with herself if she didn't admit that her first and most important love was the ranch.

Maggie knew she had inherited that oneness with the land directly from her grandfather, because it was a trait that had completely bypassed her father. Bert Holloway cared little for the ranch and the place showed it, having gone steadily downhill from the year his father died. The gradual deterioration of the once well-tended and productive cattle operation gnawed at Maggie a little more each summer, but nothing she said about it seemed to make the slightest impression on Bert.

Flicking her shoulder-length, straight-as-a-string, shiny dark hair back, Maggie turned the right signal light on and let up on the gas pedal. Excitement sparked in her nearly black eyes as she swung her modest blue sedan into the ranch's private driveway.

Maggie's gaze roamed the land on either side of the half-mile driveway almost hungrily. A small herd of mixed-breed cattle grazed on her left and the pasture on her right was completely empty except for two old bulls—a sad state of affairs when, within the realm of Maggie's memory, the ranch had boasted thousands of head of cattle.

There were several ranch roads taking off from the driveway, and on impulse Maggie turned into the one that circled the house and outbuildings in a wide sweep, intending to approach the heart of the ranch from its backside. The road dipped into a gully and rounded a stand of cottonwoods. Clearing the trees, Maggie screeched the car to a halt and stared out the window in stunned amazement.

Sheep, hundreds and hundreds of sheep, were in the main pasture, a veritable sea of small woolly animals. Maggie couldn't believe her own eyes for a few moments, but gradually the reality of the scene seeped into her brain and questions formed. Whose sheep were they? Why hadn't her parents mentioned sheep on the ranch when they stopped in Bozeman? *What the hell was going on?*

Lester Scoggins would know. Stepping on the gas, Maggie drove as fast as the dusty rutted road permitted. Sheep! Damn! Who owned them? She was certain it wasn't her parents. Granddad Lyle Holloway had left a nice estate, and Maggie's share of the cash had grown in a savings account. But she knew that the balance of the money had been gradually dribbling through her father's fingers. Maggie dearly loved her parents. Yet she understood their individual weaknesses, and there was no way Bert Holloway had suddenly raised enough money to stock the ranch with that many sheep.

Besides, the Holloways were cattle people. They'd always been cattle people. Granddad Lyle must be spinning in his grave over those blasted sheep.

Ranch headquarters, the core of the Holloway spread, consisted of the main house, a bunkhouse, which hadn't been used in quite a few years, two small one-bedroom houses and a mixture of various-sized outbuildings. The buildings were scattered over five acres, with corrals tucked in between several of them and a half-acre of lawn and trees separating the main house from the business end of the ranch.

Maggie braked to an abrupt stop near the hands' housing and saw Les Scoggins amble out of the barn, apparently alerted by the sound of her car. "Howdy, Maggie," he called cheerily.

Les was somewhere in his late fifties, Maggie believed, and had the rangy, wiry body of a man who'd worked outdoors all of his life. Les had been around for a long time, long enough that Maggie liked him and felt comfortable with him. "Hello, Les." Closing the car door, Maggie went to meet Les halfway.

"Been expecting you to come along," Les said with a grin.

"It's that time of year, all right. Les, why are there sheep on the ranch?"

Les lifted his battered old hat and settled it on his head again, a gesture that Maggie was very familiar with. "Heck, they've been here about a month now, Maggie. Your dad leased the grazing rights to a fellow by the name of Sloan Prescott."

Maggie felt the color drain from her face. "You don't mean it," she mumbled. "For the entire summer?" And then the name registered. "Sloan Prescott?"

"Well, I think it's for all summer," Les replied, frowning as if he'd just realized he really didn't know the terms of the lease. "Prescott's from Wyoming."

Suddenly feeling weak, Maggie glanced around. The place looked a little more run-down than the last time she'd seen it, which she'd expected. Every building needed repairs and a new coat of paint. The fences sagged, poles were missing from the corrals, weeds had sprung up along fencelines, around tree trunks and the buildings. The whole place had a seedy look that made Maggie want to cry. When her grandfather had been alive and healthy, the ranch had been a showplace, sparkling clean and in perfect condition.

"Sloan Prescott," she whispered, as if the name was a final blow.

"Want some help with your luggage?" Les asked.

Retreating from disorganized, unsettling memories, Maggie shook her head. "I can manage, Les, thanks. I don't have that much." She started for the car, intending to drive it closer to the house. "Oh, how's Rebel?" she asked, turning back to Les.

"Just fine. He's out in the east pasture with the other horses."

"Dad said you were taking care of him. I appreciate it."

"Aw, heck, there's not that much to do around here anymore, Maggie."

Maggie's eyebrow went up. "There's not? It looks to me
like there's a lot that needs doing."

Les scratched the front of his blue chambray shirt. "Well,
I do what your dad tells me to do."

"I know." She sighed. "I'm not blaming you, Les."

Maggie felt her high spirits take a decided drop over the
sheep and the Prescott name, and seeing the disrepair and
neglect of the place again influenced her mood, too. Dejectedly she got back in the car and drove up to the house.

After carrying her luggage into the house and upstairs to
her bedroom, Maggie sat on the bed. How could her father
have leased the land to a sheepman? Bert couldn't know
how his daughter felt about Sloan Prescott, but he should
have had at least a little consideration for the traditions and
standards of the Holloways who'd come before him. He
didn't, though. The ranch meant next to nothing to Robert
Holloway, Maggie acknowledged again while wiping a tear
from the corner of her eye. She'd always tried not to judge
her father, but she was an intelligent adult with a good many
of her grandfather's steady, down-to-earth traits. And it was
impossible not to see Bert's track record as rather sad.

He'd chosen to study law in college and then failed as a
practicing attorney. He'd tried various other ventures—from
fishing guide to building log homes to sell—and had failed
with them, too. The ranch's neglected state was evidence of
another failure.

Now he was chasing a state senate seat, and Sarah, Maggie's mother, followed wherever her husband led. Sarah
Holloway was a timid woman who wouldn't dream of
questioning anything her husband did. Maggie knew her
parents had one of the great marriages of all time, but she
suspected it was because Sarah didn't have the gumption to
bite butter, and let her husband walk all over her.

Bert walked on anyone who let him, and Maggie and her father clashed every so often. Still, they had a good relationship because Bert was the kind of person who blustered and threw his weight around, but when the smoke cleared he was all smiles again.

Maggie stared at the telephone on the bedstand, and after a moment she dug through her purse and came up with the telephone number her parents had given her during their stay in Bozeman. "We'll be barnstorming the state," Bert had proudly announced. "But if you need to reach us, Mag, call this number and they'll know where to find us."

She couldn't let this pass, Maggie realized. She wanted to hear from her father's own lips how he could have leased Holloway land to a sheepman. And she was hurt and angry enough to tell Bert just what she thought of it, too. If it was a question of money, he could have leased the land to cattle people. Good grazing land could always be leased out. Bert hadn't had to make a deal with a damned sheepman.

It took three long-distance calls, but finally Maggie heard her father's voice on the line. There was a lot of background noise, she noted, as if he was in a room with a crowd of people. "Dad?"

"Maggie? Is anything wrong?"

"I just got to the ranch a little while ago."

"Are you okay?"

"I'm fine."

"Then make this short, honey. I'm in the middle of a meeting. You could talk to your mother at the hotel—"

"No, Dad. I want to talk to you. It's about the sheep."

"The sheep? What about them?"

"Why are they here?"

"I leased the grazing rights."

"I know that. But why to a sheepman? You know how Granddad felt about sheep."

"You called me out of a meeting for that? Maggie, I don't have time for this now. Call me tonight at the hotel. Or better yet, call your mother. She can tell you—"

"Dammit, I don't want to talk to Mother! I don't understand how you could have done such a thing."

"You're upset."

"I most certainly am. How binding is that lease?"

"It's a standard form. Read it. I believe it's in my desk in the study. Maggie, I've got to go. You're home for the summer. Do anything you want with the ranch. You have my blessing and permission."

"I do? You mean you wouldn't care if I found a way to get rid of those sheep?"

A note of impatience entered Bert's voice. "Do anything you want. I doubt if your mother and I will ever live on the ranch again."

"You don't mean that."

"I most assuredly do mean that. I see a bright political future for Robert Holloway, Mag. By the way, if you get tired of hanging around there, you're very welcome to join your mother and me on the campaign trail this summer. Family support means a lot to voters, you know."

"Dad, you have my support. And anything I can do locally, I'd be glad to do. But I really want to spend the summer right here."

"Well, whatever you say. And I really mean what I said about doing what you want with the ranch. I've got to go now. I'll tell your mother you called."

An uncertain excitement was churning Maggie's insides when she put the phone down. Do what she wanted with the ranch? Wasn't that a distant hope she'd avoided putting into distinct thoughts or words? She'd always known she would inherit the ranch one day, but only after her parents' demise, which she certainly had never looked forward to. Having control now was a dream come true.

Unless this was only another of Bert Holloway's almost constant aberrations from what most people considered a normal life-style. Dare she believe him? More to the point, dare she believe his romance with politics would last?

As she unpacked her suitcases Maggie gave the subject serious thought. But pro and con arguments on the matter weren't that cut-and-dried. Not when she *wanted* to believe Bert had just given her carte blanche with the ranch. The entire subject was so heavily overlaid with emotion. And ambition. Just look at the dozens of obvious chores that needed doing around the place.

Every summer Maggie had done what she could, and while Bert hadn't openly opposed her efforts, just his attitude and presence had been a deterrent. Now she had months alone... and Bert's blessing, besides.

She could move mountains in three months, she realized thoughtfully. And what if Bert was completely sincere? What if he really had washed his hands of the place? Dare she think beyond the end of summer?

With the last blouse hung in the closet, Maggie skipped from the room and descended the stairs two at a time. She went directly to the study and sat at the large oak desk. Its top was littered and its drawers crammed with papers of every description, and it took a few minutes to locate the grazing lease. But she finally found it and sat back to read it.

As Bert had declared, it was a standard form, a pre-printed form with spaces for names and dates. Sloan Prescott, with a Wyoming address and telephone number, had been given permission to graze sheep from May first through the last day of September on Holloway land. The form was signed, dated and notarized.

Sloan Prescott. The name leaped out at Maggie as if it was written in red ink. She hadn't really thought of Sloan in years, but now he was firmly lodged in her brain. It had been what, ten years, eleven, since that dance? Maggie frowned as the memory of an uninvited and sizzling kiss dimmed her surroundings. For a moment she was eighteen again, wearing a pink froth of a dress, dancing, laughing, joking with friends.

One of those friends, Helen White, had been dating Sloan. Ten or twelve young people had been outside, catching a breath of fresh air between dances. Suddenly Sloan was there, joining the group without Helen. Maggie's opinion of Prescott was that he was handsome, but never someone she could be interested in, even if he wasn't involved with a friend. Sloan's irrevocable sin was that his family were Wyoming sheepherders.

Sitting at her father's desk, Maggie gave her head a shake. She didn't need to relive every second of that night to recapture the anger it had ended with. And she forced her attention back on the lease.

It was too legal to get around, Maggie realized with a sinking sensation. Her only chance of removing those nasty little animals from Holloway land was a personal appeal to Sloan. The idea didn't thrill her, far from it, but how else could she explain that she was taking over the ranch for the summer—and possibly indefinitely—and found a herd of sheep too much to deal with?

This was a cattle ranch, and Sloan or any other sheepman wouldn't find her distaste of the situation that unusual. What had been unusual was Bert's disloyal-to-family-tradition attitude.

Sighing, Maggie reached for the phone. She couldn't dive into the repairs and painting until she found out just how adamant Sloan was going to be about the lease.

The Prescott ranch was thirty miles into Wyoming. Sloan Prescott had readily agreed to a seven o'clock meeting that evening and given Maggie directions, with neither of them even hinting that they'd known each other before. Maggie had been prepared for some kind of familiarity, but she'd taken her cue from Sloan, and as he hadn't mentioned the past, neither had she.

She decided during the drive that Sloan had probably purposely ignored the old episode. Maggie recalled hearing at some point in the past ten years that Sloan had gotten married. Not to Helen White. Maggie had completely lost track of Helen, but she remembered rumors that Sloan had married a city gal, someone from back east. No doubt he preferred forgetting that he'd once kissed the woman who'd telephoned for a business meeting.

Or maybe he truly had forgotten the incident, Maggie mused, and then realized that possibility gave her an odd pang. Which was rather silly. She'd all but forgotten Sloan until today, and why should he remember her?

His place had the same crisply-cared-for look that the Holloway ranch used to have, Maggie noted when she drove up to the house. The grounds were neat and attractive with flowers, shrubbery and trees, the fences were arrow-straight and taut, and the outbuildings were all painted in the same bluish-gray and white pattern that coordinated with the paint on the old but sturdy-looking two-story house. Sheep by the thousands dotted the fenced pastures surrounding the ranch buildings, and the whole place had an air of affluence and serene beauty.

She could make the Holloway ranch just as beautiful, Maggie determined as she stopped the car beside a black pickup truck. The sun was still up but waning in the western sky, casting long shadows across the Prescott lawn, and the evening had a lovely, hushed quality. Maggie followed a strip of cement sidewalk to the front porch steps and, adjusting her shoulder bag a tad nervously, climbed the stairs, crossed the porch and pressed the button for the doorbell.

"I'm coming," rang from within the house, and in a moment the door swung open.

Maggie stared. The man at the door was unmistakably Sloan Prescott, a more mature Sloan Prescott, to be sure, but he was as lean and good-looking as he'd been ten years ago. His hair was thick and dark, that rich color between black and brown, and his eyes were a bright, piercing blue. He had a nice nose, a strong jaw and a wonderfully masculine mouth. Wearing jeans, polished black boots and a shirt the color of old ivory, he was astonishingly handsome, actually taking Maggie's breath away.

She found her wits and a voice. "I'm Maggie Holloway."

Sloan was staring, too. Maggie hadn't had to introduce herself. He remembered her very well. He was a hardworking rancher, and a business meeting with a woman was only another business meeting. He'd been married and divorced and had had an awful lot of reserve around women ever since.

But this was Maggie Holloway standing at his door, and he couldn't stop filling his eyes. The years had been kind to her. Maturity only enhanced her striking dark hair and eyes, and the off-white slacks and blouse she was wearing emphasized her slender build, long legs and the natural gold tint of her skin.

"Hello, Maggie. Come in."

He recognized her! She could see it in his eyes. Maggie felt a strange giddiness all of a sudden. "Thank you." Peering around the foyer and then the hall that Sloan led her through, Maggie realized she was looking for signs of a family, a wife, children. She saw or heard nothing in that regard, and by the quiet of the house, she could only presume that she and Sloan were completely alone. It struck Maggie as odd and she wondered about those old rumors.

They ended up in a comfortable room with a desk, leather furniture in front of a large rock fireplace and lots of bookshelves on the walls. "Thank you for meeting me on such short notice," Maggie said.

"No problem. Let's sit over here." Sloan went to the leather couch and Maggie chose a matching chair. When they were settled, Sloan smiled, giving Maggie a rather startling sensation in the pit of her stomach. His smile was incredible, and she thought of that long-ago kiss and wondered if it was in his mind, too. "Now, what did you want to see me about?" she heard Sloan say.

Maggie cleared her throat. Apparently Sloan wasn't dwelling on the past like she was, for which she felt some gratitude. That incident really was best forgotten in light of their present situation. "I would like to discuss the grazing lease my father gave you," she said clearly.

Sloan nodded agreeably. "What about it?"

"Well, it surprised me, for one thing. I'm sure you understand that the Holloways have always been cattle people, and when I saw sheep on the place..." Maggie's voice trailed off. With Sloan a sheepman, he fully understood the old animosities between "sheepers" and cattlemen. And if he remembered their run-in ten years ago, he also remembered where she stood on the issue.

Still, that old prejudice wasn't a strong enough reason for requesting he agree to dissolve the grazing agreement. Maggie's chin came up a trifle. "I'm going to be running the ranch now, Sloan, and I have different plans for the place than my father did."

Sloan cocked an eyebrow. "You're going to stock heavily enough that you'll need all that grass?"

"Well..." Embarrassment deepened Maggie's color. Her plans were so vague yet. Other than some much needed repairs to the place, did she even have any real plans?

"Maggie, where were you when your dad and I agreed on the lease?"

"In Bozeman. I teach at the university."

"I see." Getting to his feet, Sloan made a circle of the room. He stopped at the fireplace. "Let me get this straight. You came here with the hope that I would agree to cancel the lease?"

"That's what I came to discuss, yes. I would return your money, of course."

Sloan waved the topic aside. "Money's not the problem. I have no other place to put those sheep for the summer. Any suggestions on where I could move six hundred sheep if I agreed to tear up that lease?"

Maggie's shoulders slumped. She hadn't presented a good case. Actually she hadn't even *prepared* a good case. She had no reason but emotion for wanting those sheep off Holloway land, and she could see that Sloan wasn't a man who functioned on emotion. "No, I have no suggestions," she admitted huskily. "But I want them moved. My grandfather detested sheep."

"Your grandfather?"

"He's dead. But I still respect his feelings."

"You're living in the past, Maggie. Most sheepmen and cattlemen get along just fine today. Some ranchers raise both. You have to know that."

Her eyes sparked. "Not all of them get along," she rebutted sharply.

"No, there are a few ranchers scattered around who cling to the old ways. But I'm not one of them, and I'm rather surprised that you are. Your father doesn't feel that way."

"My father..." Maggie stopped herself. Blurting out her sorrow and resentment that Bert Holloway's concern for the ranch would fit on the head of a pin would accomplish nothing. "My father and I have differing opinions," she finished lamely.

Sloan rubbed the back of his neck thoughtfully. "We have a problem, don't we? You're asking for something damned near impossible. And it doesn't even make sense. Why should all that grass on your place go to waste?"

Behind the conversation, Maggie had been thinking some startling thoughts. She wanted the Holloway ranch, desperately wanted it. And her father didn't. Why wouldn't he agree to sell it to her? An offer to buy it would surprise him, but he could always use the payments she would agree to make. And she *could* stock the place and use that grass herself. Her inheritance had grown to a nice sum, certainly enough to make a respectable start in the cattle business. Along with the stock still on the ranch, she could be in business for sure.

This was impulsive, to be true, but maybe only saying it out loud was impulsive. The desire had always been there, smothered by other influences, but there all the same. "The grass won't go to waste. I plan to start stocking the ranch immediately."

Instinct told Sloan that Maggie had just now reached that decision, and he wondered what sort of agreement she and Bert had come to on their ranch. "Beef isn't a sure profit anymore. Maybe you should consider sheep," he suggested, sincere in his opinion that sheep were the better risk.

"Sheep!" Maggie scoffed without a second's hesitation. "I wouldn't run sheep for any amount of profit."

"Because of your grandfather?" he asked in a mildly amused tone.

Maggie's cheeks got darker. "Don't make fun of my feelings for my grandfather. Did you know him?"

"No, I never had that honor."

"Then you couldn't possibly understand the kind of man he was."

Sloan studied her intently. "Still, this is another age, Maggie. Are you planning to operate that ranch like he did, with his values and ethics?"

"I could do worse. The Holloway ranch was once as commanding and attractive as this one is. That was during my grandfather's lifetime."

"I see." Frowning, Sloan paced again. It was apparent that Maggie Holloway still clung to the same old prejudice that she'd lit into him with ten years ago. He was pro-sheep; she was pro-cattle. In her mind, the breach was irreconcilable. It was a silly feud, but, like they'd already discussed, Maggie and he weren't the only ranchers involved in it.

When Sloan stopped again, it was with a negative head shake. "I'm sorry, Maggie, but I can't cancel the lease. My summer program is all set and in motion. I need that pasture for my animals."

Maggie slowly rose. "And *my* animals? What should I do with the stock I'll be bringing in?"

"Maybe you'll just have to delay your plans."

Maggie had guarded against anger. She had vowed repeatedly on the thirty-mile drive to keep cool no matter what took place at the Prescott ranch. But Sloan stating that she should delay buying stock just so his sheep could eat *her* grass was too much. "You're a very self-assured man, aren't you?" she said caustically. "What do you know about me and my plans? Or what led up to this meeting? My family's ranch is suddenly within my reach, and not you or anyone else is going to prevent me from going forward with it."

"I admire your spunk, Maggie."

"Oh, I can see that. You're thinking that I'm some kind of a nut case." Her eyes narrowed. "I'm as good a rancher as you are, and I'll prove it, too. Your sheep will be a hindrance, but they won't be a delay. I'll find a way to deal with the problem, and that's a promise."

Why, she was furious, Sloan finally realized in amazement. She wasn't screaming and yelling, but she was positively furious. "Why are you so mad?" he asked. "There's no reason we can't be friends."

"No reason! Now, *that's* funny." Turning, Maggie started for the door.

"Wait a minute! Don't go off mad. Let's talk about this." Sloan took three long strides and caught Maggie's shoulder.

She spun around, with fingernails poised and teeth bared. Startled, Sloan grabbed her wrists. "What the hell's wrong with you? Calm down!"

"Let go of me, you damned...damned sheeper!"

Sloan had to laugh, in spite of her fury. "Is that the worst name you can think of to call me? I don't happen to think that's an insult, Maggie." He held her wrists and stared into the dark, velvety depths of her eyes, and something rippled within him. Desire, strong and hot, was spreading through his system, just like it had that night ten years ago. Maggie Holloway might be a nut case, but she was a sexy nut case.

It had been a long time since a woman had moved him this way. A bad marriage and divorce had diminished Sloan's interest in the opposite sex, and most of the time he went about his daily chores without ever thinking of women. Now this fiery handful had intruded on his life, demanding a ridiculous concession and lighting fires he'd been success-ful at keeping low and banked. It was damned annoy-ing...but also damned exciting...and his gaze landed on her mouth.

Maggie sucked in a sharp breath. Something was going on behind those blue eyes, and she was almost afraid to put a name to it. "Let go of me," she whispered.

"Yeah, I will. In a minute. Are you married?"

"My God, no. What's that go—"

"Neither am I." Sloan moved fast, releasing her wrists and hauling her up against himself in one fluid movement. His mouth crashed down on hers before Maggie could even yelp, and with her eyes wide open in stunned disbelief, she found herself being thoroughly kissed. In the confusion of her brain, she remembered that other kiss, and remem-bered, too, that it had come as fast and unexpectedly as this one.

Sloan's leanness was still deceiving, she realized numbly, because his arms were like steel bands around her, just like before. And his body was hard and unyielding, a fortress of firm flesh keeping her in place. His mouth moved on hers, asking for participation. Her breasts were squashed into his chest, and he was holding her close enough for her to feel much too much of his anatomy below his belt.

Her pulse beat was going crazy, her stomach tense and achy before he raised his head. "How dare you?" she quaked hoarsely. "I can see you haven't changed one iota!"

Sloan took a shaky breath. "That's some chemistry, honey. That hasn't changed, either. It was between us ten years ago, and it's still between us."

"Don't you dare 'honey' me, you...you barbarian! Is this how you ordinarily treat women who come to your house to discuss business?"

A frown creased Sloan's forehead. "Women don't come to my house to discuss business." He couldn't believe he'd kissed Maggie again. But he had, and she felt like she belonged in his arms. That was the hardest part of this crazy thing to digest. Maggie Holloway felt like she *belonged* right where she was. What's more, he'd like to lead her upstairs to his bedroom, or—what the hell?—make love to her right here, on the floor, on the couch, where didn't really matter. One minute they'd been talking—or arguing—and the next minute he'd forced a kiss. Again. How did she have the power to make him behave like a sex-starved cretin?

Sloan relaxed his arms and stepped back. "I'm sorry," he mumbled, not quite meeting Maggie's eyes.

With her hands and legs trembling, Maggie turned to the door again. She marched out of the room and out of the house without looking back, not even wanting to think of what had just happened until she was in her car and off the Prescott ranch.

Two

"We need to talk about something, Les," Maggie announced the next morning. She'd put in a bad night, what with Sloan Prescott and sheep haunting her dreams. But with the sun, she was again determined to at least make a brave attempt to fulfill her hopes for the ranch.

"Sure, Maggie," Les agreed with a grin.

"Well, with Dad's permission, I'm taking over the ranch."

"You? How come?"

"I'm hoping to make a deal with Dad and Mother to buy it. Dad doesn't want to live here anymore."

Les rubbed his jaw. "Well, I'll be da . . . danged," he remarked, obviously taken aback.

"Anyway, whatever happens in that regard, I intend to use this summer to get the place in shape. I'd like you to stay and help me, but I'll understand if you don't want to dive in and work from morning till night. That's what it's going to take, a lot of hard work." They were standing in the yard, and Maggie's troubled gaze swept the compound. "There's so much that needs doing," she murmured.

"Well, gosh, Maggie, this place is home to me. Where would I go? Sure, I'll stay."

Maggie smiled with relief and thanks. "I was hoping you would."

Les did his little routine with his hat. "So, what d'ya want done first?"

As it happened Maggie was at that moment glaring at a two-foot-high thistle. "Let's get rid of those darned weeds. They're driving me crazy."

Les laughed out loud. "Sure thing. I'll go dig out the tools."

"I'm going in to make some phone calls, then I'll be out to help." Maggie headed for the house while Les ambled toward one of the sheds. Inside, she went to the study, sat at the desk and opened the telephone book. Finding the number she wanted, Maggie dialed and heard, "Lawson's Auction House."

"Hello. I'd like to know the date of your next scheduled Black Angus auction." Maggie had decided that if her parents agreed to sell her the ranch, she wanted to stock it with Black Angus cattle. They were a good breed, more expensive than what the ranch now raised, but she intended getting started on the right foot.

After a brief pause the man on the phone said, "A week from this Wednesday, ma'am. Are you buying or selling?"

"Buying. What time will the auction start?"

"Ten in the morning."

"Thank you." Maggie made a notation on the desk calendar and sat back. She had a little over a week to approach her parents with a purchase offer. But she wanted to get her mother's viewpoint on Bert's resolution about never living on the place again before she went ahead with her plans. Deciding that was the best course, Maggie dialed the hotel in Helena where Bert and Sarah were staying.

Sarah answered the room ring with a pleasant, "Hello. This is Sarah Holloway."

"This is Maggie, Mother. How are you?"

"Just fine, dear. How are you? Dad said you called yesterday."

"I called about the sheep on the ranch. Dad's rather blasé about them, isn't he?"

"Well, you know your father, dear."

"Yes, I do. Mother, he mentioned how well everything is going for the two of you in the campaign. Do you feel that way, too?"

"Of course I do. Why, dear?"

"You do understand that he's not planning to live on the ranch again."

"He's mentioned it several times, yes. Why, Maggie?"

"Living elsewhere wouldn't bother you?"

"Wherever your father wants to live is fine with me, dear."

Maggie smiled rather grimly over the predictable statement. "Dad gave me permission to take over the ranch's operation. Did he tell you that?"

"Why, I'm not sure. He's been very busy, Maggie. Goodness, do you *want* to take over? Whatever for, dear? That old place is in terrible shape."

"Old place? Mother, this has been our home, *your* home for many years. Don't you have some affection for the ranch?"

Sarah's voice was rather vague. "Well, I suppose I do. But if your father wants to live elsewhere—"

"I understand, Mother," Maggie interjected quietly. "Well, tell Dad I said hello, and I'll call again in a few days."

"We'll be in Great Falls in a few days, Maggie. Two days there and then on to Kalispel for two more days."

"I'll reach you through the number you gave me, Mother. Good-bye."

Maggie put the phone down and laid her head back against the high back of the desk chair. She stared at the ceiling as the conversations, with Bert yesterday and Sarah just now, replayed in her mind. Each parent seemed totally unconcerned about the ranch, and it made Maggie sad to realize how little feeling her parents had for a place she felt so tied to.

Why was she so different from her own mother and father? She'd been a lot more in tune with her grandfather than she'd ever been with Bert and Sarah. Her childhood days of following Granddad Lyle around were wonderful memories. She'd ridden with him, too, honing her mastery of western horsemanship. He'd had a little jingle to make her laugh, one he'd chanted like the Munchkins in the *Wizard of Oz* movie. Only instead of singing, "Follow the yellow brick road," Lyle Holloway had sung, "Working the Holloway way." He'd made chores fun with that silly jingle.

Sighing with nostalgia, Maggie turned her thoughts to last night and Sloan Prescott. The man had a nerve, that's for sure. He'd *always* had a nerve. But he had something else, something she didn't want to even get close to again—a whole lot of magnetism. Oh, yes, she was much too honest to pretend she hadn't felt something during that kiss. Actually she'd felt quite a lot, even if she'd have died before letting on. She hadn't let on ten years ago, either, but her traitorous body had responded to Sloan's kiss then, as well.

And he'd made it very clear he was no longer married. Why?

Maggie put her face in her hands. No way was she going to get personally involved with a sheepman! There were some loyalties just too meaningful to tamper with, and this was one of them. Why, if Lyle Holloway was still alive and thought that his granddaughter would even look at a sheeper, he'd thunder and roar around like an enraged bull. Lyle hadn't had any ethnic or religious prejudices, but where sheep were concerned, he'd pulled no punches. Maggie wouldn't even repeat some of the things she remembered her grandfather saying about sheepmen.

Of course, she'd grown up with an entirely different image of sheepers than what Sloan Prescott projected. But just because he wasn't whiskery and dirty and living in a horrible little trailer in the hills with his sheep milling around, didn't make him any less a sheepherder.

How had he dared kiss her again? And after refusing to tear up the lease, too!

Every time Maggie saw Sloan's sheep on Holloway land that morning, anger and resentment flared up again. She dug and hacked at weeds right along with Les until noon, then, wiping the sweat off of her forehead with the sleeve of her shirt, she called a lunch break. "Come on up to the house and I'll put something together, Les," she invited.

"No, thanks. I'll go have my beans. You can join me if you want to, though," he added with a teasing grin, knowing full well that Maggie had tried his "beans" years ago and had nearly choked to death. Les's recipe contained jalapeño peppers, *lots* of jalapeño peppers.

"I'm surprised you have any insides left after eating those things for so many years," Maggie said with a laugh and a shake of her head. "See you in about an hour, okay?"

She was almost to the back door of the house when she heard Les yell out, "Here comes Prescott."

"What?" Startled, Maggie went to the corner of the house to get a look at the long driveway. Sure enough, the black pickup she'd seen parked beside Sloan's house last night was kicking up dust. She turned and shouted, "Does he come around here very often?"

"Yeah," Les yelled. "Every few days to check on his herd."

Frowning, Maggie watched the pickup for a minute, then felt relief when it turned off on the same road she'd followed yesterday. At least the man didn't have to come near the house to check on his damned sheep.

Going into the house, Maggie headed straight for the bathroom. She was hot and sweaty, and it felt wonderful to wash her face and neck with cool water. Refreshed, she brushed her hair and gave her appearance a once-over. Her working clothes consisted of faded, nearly worn-out jeans and a red T-shirt. When she rode Rebel she wore boots, but today she was wearing a pair of old sneakers, and all in all, her outfit looked pretty disreputable.

But she hadn't invited Sloan Prescott to the ranch, and if he should happen to stop at the house he'd have to accept her the way she was, or not at all. It was all the same to her.

In the kitchen, Maggie opened the refrigerator and stared at the nearly empty shelves. There was lots of food in the big freezer in the utility room, but with her parents having been gone for weeks before she arrived, it was only natural that the refrigerator would be practically empty. She was going to have to make a grocery run into town very soon, she realized, and closed the refrigerator to make an inspection of the canned goods in the pantry.

Deciding on vegetable soup, Maggie took the can to the kitchen and began a search through the cutlery drawer for the can opener. The sound of a motor brought her up short. "Uh, oh," she muttered, and went to a window overlooking the driveway.

Sloan pulled the pickup to a stop, cut the engine and climbed out. He wasn't sure why he was there, or rather, he didn't want to admit a desire to see Maggie Holloway again. Yet something stronger than his longtime pattern of avoiding possibly troublesome women had turned the truck toward her house, and that same something was directing his long legs to her back door. It swung open before he could knock, and he blinked at the cold, what-do-*you*-want expression on Maggie's face.

"Hi," he said softly, and glanced down to the can she was holding. "Having lunch?"

"Something I can do for you?" Maggie asked coolly, completely ignoring his stab at amiability.

Sloan, in turn, ignored her rudeness. "We could have lunch in town. That's why I came by," he lied, relieved to have come up with an excuse for stopping like this. "I'm on my way to Newley for lunch and—"

"Don't be absurd," Maggie snapped. "I have no intention of going anywhere with you, especially to Newley where everyone knows me."

"Oh. You don't want to be seen with a sheepman."

"Does that surprise you?"

"Actually, it does. I find that attitude a little strange in an educated person. Didn't you say you taught at the university in Bozeman?"

"My attitude wasn't part of my college curriculum, Sloan. It was learned at my grandfather's knee, and I have no reason *or* desire to change it."

Sloan shifted his weight from one booted foot to the other. "It's a pretty narrow attitude, Maggie." His gaze lingered on the mouth he'd kissed twice now, then dropped to the red T-shirt she was wearing. She was lean and lithe, with small, firm breasts poking knobs into the red fabric. Her old jeans fit so well they were wrinkleless, and the shape of her legs, her thighs, particularly, was giving him that same feeling he'd had with Maggie last night.

Clearing his throat, Sloan looked away. Her hair was too shiny, her eyes too striking, her body too sexy, for him to stand there and not notice them, and more. She exuded an indistinct invitation, a femaleness that she couldn't help, and he couldn't help responding to.

Shaking his head to clear it, Sloan backed away from the door. He didn't want this any more than Maggie did. What the hell was he doing here? "Well, I guess there's no point in debating attitudes, is there?'' he mumbled, and stepped off the small back porch.

"None that I can see." Slightly puzzled, Maggie watched Sloan practically run back to his pickup. Then, giving the door a push closed, she plopped down on the nearest kitchen chair and listened to him driving away. "What was that all about?" she muttered, positive that Sloan had had second thoughts about something or other.

Well, she'd set him straight about any possible socializing. And she was glad she'd had the opportunity to do so.

Maggie got to her feet and went back to the cutlery drawer to resume her search for that elusive can opener.

For five days straight Maggie and Les worked from dawn until dusk. Her only breaks were trips to Newley for supplies—food and paint and brushes and lumber and fence posts and barbed wire. She borrowed Les's rickety old pickup for the trips, and hurried through them, ever anxious to get back to the ranch and whatever project the shopping foray had interrupted.

She was extraordinarily keyed up, she realized, with the proposal to buy the ranch never far from her thoughts. During another telephone conversation with her mother, Maggie had learned that her parents were spending the following weekend on a ranch in the northwestern part of the state. "A weekend of leisure," Sarah had told her. "Your father is running himself ragged with speeches and meetings. He needs a few days off."

Maggie had immediately seen the opportunity for broaching the subject of the ranch purchase, and had asked for the telephone number of the distant ranch so she could call on Sunday afternoon. "To discuss an important matter with both you and Dad, Mother."

Sarah had been curious, but Maggie had sidestepped her questions with assurances that she would call on Sunday afternoon.

On Sunday morning Maggie decided to go to church. Les had the day off, and she figured an hour of devotion would calm her nerves and give her a chance to say hello to some old friends. Up early as usual, Maggie had time to give herself a manicure before getting ready for church. Her nails had taken a beating the past week, but she filed and shaped them as best she could, before applying a coat of clear polish.

Concentrating on the task, it was a few minutes before she realized Sloan Prescott had seeped into her thoughts again. His black pickup was around too often for her to completely forget the man, even if his damned sheep weren't a constant reminder. But after that one time, Sloan had avoided the house. Which was fine with Maggie. She wanted nothing to do with Prescott.

But still, she found herself thinking about him and remembering his kisses—both of them, even if they were ten years apart—much too often. She wasn't a prude or a moralist. She dealt with her own sexuality without any Victorian hangups, and it wasn't the fact that she'd been kissed again that upset her: it was the man who'd administered it. The plain truth, she finally had to admit, was that if Sloan was anyone else but the owner of those blasted sheep that were eating her grass, she would like him. Even with that old incident involving Helen White an uneasy memory, Maggie would like him.

The less contact she had with Sloan, the better off she'd be, Maggie reaffirmed. He had a little too much sexual power for her to be chancing *any* kind of a relationship with him, even an antagonistic one.

Maggie put on a dress and mid-heeled pumps for church. The dress was a simple blue and white summer print and the pumps and her handbag were plain white, a nice, going-to-church outfit. But after a week of jeans, sneakers and ratty old T-shirts, she felt dressed up, and drove away anticipating a pleasant morning.

* * *

Maggie felt peaceful on the drive back to the ranch. The church service had been comforting, and afterward she'd enjoyed visiting with friends she hadn't seen in some time. She'd also gathered a little information, although she hadn't actively sought all of it.

Her old friend Helen White had been on her mind sporadically since running into Sloan again, and when Maggie spotted an aunt of Helen's after church, she asked Esther Soderham where Helen lived these days. Esther had seemed delighted to report that Helen had moved to Denver some years back, had married a nice fellow and had three children. Maggie asked for and received Helen's telephone number and address, and planned to drop her former classmate a line. And not because of Sloan, either, she told herself. People were too careless with friendships. She would sincerely enjoy contact with Helen again.

The other information she'd picked up hadn't been intentionally sought. It was about Sloan. A group of her parents' friends asked how Bert and Sarah were doing in the campaign, and once past those amenities, someone mentioned the sheep on the Holloway ranch. One thing led to another after that, and Maggie found herself listening to a few references to Sloan on a personal level. The consensus of opinion, Maggie discovered, was that sheepman or not, in essentially cattle country, Sloan was well-liked, while his wife hadn't been.

At that point Maggie had to literally clench her teeth to keep from prying. Sloan's ex-wife was none of her business, but there was no doubting the burning curiosity her well-meaning but talkative friends had aroused.

The day was warm from a bright sun and a clear sky, and the fields Maggie was driving past were a vivid green. Later in the summer those same fields would turn to a drab, dry-looking tan, but in June their moist verdancy was almost luminous.

Putting Sloan out of her mind, Maggie concentrated on just the right verbiage to present her offer to her parents that afternoon. She turned into the ranch driveway and within seconds spotted Sloan's pickup coming toward her. He'd obviously made another check of his herd and was leaving. For just a moment a strange confusion hit Maggie: should she drive on by without even a wave?

The question was moot, she realized when the black pickup stopped squarely in the middle of the narrow road, giving her no room to drive by. Sighing impatiently, she braked and moved the shifting lever into park.

Sloan got out of his truck and came up to Maggie's open window. He bent over to see in. "Hello."

"Hello." She sent him only a brief side-glance, but felt his gaze wandering over the blue and white dress.

"Been to church?"

"As a matter of fact, yes."

"I was wondering if you'd like to take a ride."

"A ride where?"

"A horseback ride. I'm going up into the mountains. Why don't you come along?"

Lord, she'd love a long ride. In her haste to get the ranch in better shape, she'd all but neglected Rebel. The few rides she had taken had been short evening spurts, when she hadn't been too tired to do more than fall into bed. But she had that phone call to make, and besides, spending an afternoon with Sloan Prescott was neither smart, nor part of her planned agenda. "Sorry, I have other things I have to do."

"You do ride, don't you?"

Maggie gave him an openmouthed smirk, then drawled disdainfully, "Yes, Sloan, I do ride. I grew up on this ranch, you know."

His eyes contained amusement. "Oh, I know you used to be a cowgirl, honey. I just wondered if you still were."

"*All* the Holloways have been cow-people, so if you're trying to give me a little slam along with that smile, you're wasting your time."

"Slam? Maggie, you've got me all wrong. Why would I slam a woman who looks good enough to eat?"

He was flirting, Maggie realized, and flushed a little. He wanted a lot more from her than just a concession on his sheep. That's why he'd asked her to lunch that day and why he'd just now asked her to take a ride with him.

She had absorbed, even without trying, the blue, match-his-eyes shirt he was wearing, and the way he'd tipped his Stetson to the back of his head, freeing a lock of dark hair to drape down over the right side of his forehead. Maggie couldn't deny that he was a handsome specimen of mankind, totally male, confident that he belonged right where he was in the world.

He probably had any woman he snapped his fingers at doing flips, Maggie thought resentfully, determining not to join those particular ranks. But again questions formed about his ex-wife. Maggie realized that she did not want to get involved with Sloan. He was a dangerous man, too sexy, and they had to coexist within the structure of that despicable lease. Anything beyond that wasn't sensible, not when they were each so firmly entrenched on opposite sides of that old fence.

Maggie's voice was cool and controlled, and she saw no reason to be anything but completely candid. "I have no intention of sitting here and flirting with you, Sloan. Please move your pickup. I'd like to go on to the house."

This had been a spur-of-the-moment impulse for Sloan, and he was sorry he'd given Maggie the opportunity to turn him down again. He didn't behave normally around her, and it irritated the hell out of him every time he did it. Even so, he'd like to jerk her out of that car and kiss her breathless, and it astounded him that he was developing so much desire for a woman who made no bones about her dislike of him.

All he could do was bow out gracefully. "Sure, glad to," he drawled, and with a mocking salute, walked away.

Frowning, Maggie watched him get back in his truck. Sloan drove around her car with another little salute and sped away, but it was at least a full minute before she put the shift back into drive and got moving again.

"Dad, Mother, I have something very important to talk over with you both." Maggie heard assenting sounds through the telephone, and plunged into her proposition. "I want to buy the ranch from you."

Both parents started talking at once, neither of which Maggie could understand. Finally, and to be expected, Sarah gave Bert the floor. "What are you talking about?" he demanded.

"I'm talking about a legal purchase, Dad. I want the ranch, and you and Mother don't. I would make monthly, quarterly or annual payments, whichever you'd prefer."

"We're talking about a large sum of money, Maggie," Bert cautioned.

"I know we are. Judging from the prices of two other ranches for sale in the area, I would estimate we're talking somewhere in the two hundred to three hundred thousand dollar range. I won't argue price, Dad. Whatever you think the ranch is worth, that's what I'll pay."

"Oh, dear," Sarah got in. "Maggie, you shouldn't have to pay for something that will be yours one day, anyway. Isn't that right, Bert?"

"Of course, it's right. This is the silliest thing I've ever heard of," Bert scoffed. "Maggie, aren't you being a little foolhardy here? I know you've saved your money, but you couldn't possibly have enough to be throwing it away for no reason."

"This isn't throwing it away, Dad. Not to me, it isn't. Please try to understand how much this place means to me. Les and I have been working hard on it—"

"Doing what?" Bert put in.

"General maintenance and painting. There's a cattle auction coming up that I want to attend. I'd like to get the wheels in motion on a purchase contract right away."

"Sounds like you've got big plans for the place."

"I do. Will you two please talk it over and call me back with your decision?"

"You really want to make payments on it?" Bert asked.

"I do, Dad. I want complete ownership."

"What about the university?"

"If this works out, I'll cancel my teaching contract."

"Maggie, are you really sure?" Sarah asked anxiously.

"I've never been more certain of anything in my life, Mother. If you and Dad don't plan to live on the ranch again, it's only good sense to sell it. It's a financial drain on the two of you the way it is. Well, you've got a built-in buyer. Me. Please think about it."

"We'll call you back later today," Bert promised.

Maggie stayed close to the house the rest of the day, afraid to miss her parents' call. After wandering around aimlessly for a while, she decided that busy was best and changed into jeans and got out the vacuum cleaner. The house had been dusty even at her arrival, and she hadn't taken the time from her outside activities to do any cleaning. She spent the afternoon vacuuming, dusting and scrubbing.

It was almost five o'clock when the phone rang, and she ran for it with a prayer in her heart. "Maggie? We've talked this thing to death," Bert said in her ear.

"And?"

"Well, it does make a certain amount of sense for your mother and me to sell the place if we're not going to be living there."

Maggie's heart began pounding. "Yes, it does, Dad."

"And Les's wages and other expenses are a drain, as you suggested. The ranch hasn't made a decent profit in years."

"Yes, I know, Dad."

"You're sure you want to do this?"

"Very sure."

"Maggie, you're so much like your grandfather, I can't believe it."

"I know, Dad." Maggie smiled.

"Well, if you're really sure, I guess you can go ahead with it."

An egg-sized lump in Maggie's throat was hard to swallow. "Thank you, Dad. Would you draw up the contract?"

"I'm too busy, Mag. Go see George Shipley. He'll handle it for you."

George was an attorney, an old friend practicing in Billings. "All right. About the price and terms...?"

"Whatever the going rate is will be fine on the price. As for terms, your mother and I could use monthly payments. Are you sure you can handle them, though?"

"I can handle them," Maggie breathed. "I'll go and see George tomorrow and get the wheels in motion. And thank you, Dad."

After a few words with her mother, Maggie put the phone down, then let out a loud and elated, "Yahoo!" The place was hers, to do anything she wanted with. She wouldn't worry about her parents' personal possessions around the house; they could pick and choose and take what they wanted when they got permanently settled again.

But now she could attend that auction and buy her Black Angus cattle. She could clean and paint and make plans. She could....

Oh, Lord. Those wretched sheep. They were really going to be in the way now. What was she going to do about them?

Three

――――

Maggie called George Shipley the following morning with the hope of seeing him that same day. But the attorney couldn't give her an appointment until Tuesday, so Maggie went back outside to the job she'd interrupted for the phone call.

Using a wire brush, she was scraping old scales of loose paint from one of the equipment shed's exterior walls. Les had already hammered that particular building back together and was repairing another, working near enough to yell at Maggie every so often about one subject or another. He was becoming quite enthused about getting the ranch back in shape, Maggie suspected, and she thanked her lucky stars that Les had agreed to stay. There were too many tasks that needed a man's strength.

The surprising factor of Les's willing contribution was what a good worker he was. He dove into any project Maggie set him to. But he needed direction, someone to say, "Today we're going to paint," or, "Let's lube and service the well motor today, Les." That was what he'd rarely gotten from Bert, and it was a small wonder the place wasn't in even worse shape than it was.

Les was definitely earning his pay now, Maggie thought with a faint smile while she rested her arm for a moment. Scraping paint was not an easy job.

"So, you're gonna buy Black Angus, huh?" Les called.

Maggie smiled again. They had already discussed that point several times, but Les seemed almost proud that the Holloway ranch would soon be raising Angus. "They're a good breed," she called back.

"Expensive, though."

At the sound of a motor, Maggie walked away from the shed and to a spot from which she could see the driveway. Sloan's black pickup came into view, and she wondered why he was coming to check on his sheep again today. He certainly gave his animals a lot of attention, she thought wryly.

"Is that Prescott again?" Les yelled.

"Yes," she shouted. "I thought you said he only came around every few days. He's here almost every day."

Les came down from the ladder he'd been standing on and walked toward Maggie with a broad grin. "Now, that's a fact, ain't it? Funny, before you came home he made a lot fewer visits. Maybe he's got a crush on you, Maggie."

Blushing over some good-natured teasing annoyed Maggie, maybe because she suspected Les's conjecture was true. Sloan *was* interested in her. Any woman would catch on after those invitations and too many admiring looks. And there wasn't one good reason for Sloan to check on his sheep every day. The herd was perfectly safe in Maggie's main pasture, with the ranch's best grass to eat and a four-foot-wide running creek of water to drink.

"As far as I'm concerned," she fumed, "Sloan Prescott can take his animals *and* his crush and go to Hades!" Les's laughter followed her back to the equipment shed, where she vigorously started brushing the old paint again. She finally sent the amiable hired man a sheepish smile, somewhat embarrassed that she'd let a little teasing get to her.

About ten minutes later Maggie heard Sloan's pickup pull up and stop near the house. She kept on working, refusing to give in to the impulse to look back at him. She listened though, and heard the slam of his truck door, and then barely audible footsteps becoming louder. She felt him behind her, and gritted her teeth and wielded the wire brush with a fury.

"Looks like a different place already, Maggie."

"No, it's beginning to look like it used to," she rebutted, then finally looked at him. "Something you need, Sloan?"

His blue eyes started at her sneakers and worked up her bare legs to the fringe of the cutoff jeans hitting her mid-thigh. Maggie was actually stunned by her reaction to just this man's gaze. Her skin was suddenly warmer, and she thought of something brand new to her: a body blush. Either she was getting pink all over from that sexy look or she was having a premature hot flash.

When his eyes were finally leveled on her face, he said softly, "That's a loaded question, Maggie."

Question? What question? Confused, it took Maggie a moment to recall that she'd just asked him if there was something he needed. Her expression instantly cooled, pink blush and all. "Don't play that kind of game with me. I've got more things on my mind than carrying on a silly conversation about loaded questions."

Sloan raised an amused eyebrow at her. "I guess you've pretty much dedicated your summer to hard work, right?"

"Do you find that funny?"

"Nope. I've never looked on hard work as funny." Sloan took a step closer to the building and laid a hand on the old, rough lumber siding, but his mind wasn't on how badly the building needed that coat of paint Maggie was obviously planning. "But all work and no play makes Jack a dull boy." He gave Maggie a glance. "Or Maggie a dull girl. Is that what you're aiming for, a dull summer?"

Maggie put her hands on her hips indignantly. "In the first place, I don't find working on my ranch either too hard or even slightly dull, and in the—"

"Your ranch? Your father's ranch, don't you mean?"

Her eyes glistened with pride. "I *mean* my ranch. I'm buying it from my parents. They agreed yesterday."

Sloan studied her, then looked away. "Well, I'll be damned," he said under his breath. Facing her again, in a louder voice he said, "You weren't kidding about having plans, were you? And you really are going to restock?"

"Absolutely." Maggie's gaze narrowed on him. "You know, that brings up an interesting question. I'll ask my attorney about it tomorrow."

"What question?"

"About whether or not a new owner has to honor the previous owner's commitments, of course," she replied sweetly, and rather enjoyed the surprised look on Sloan's face. It was fleeting, though.

"I'll fight you, Maggie. If you try to get out of that lease, I guarantee the whole thing will be tied up at least until the end of September."

He'd spoken positively, but with underlying amusement. The lease would expire naturally at the end of September, and one way or another, Sloan's sheep were going to be a part of her summer. Anger careened through Maggie's system. "Damn, you're irritating," she hurled without thinking.

"Because I won't lie down and let you walk on me?" Sloan's eyes narrowed, and his voice dropped a notch. "Would you like me better if I laid down and let you walk on me, Maggie?"

There was so much innuendo in the question, Maggie flushed again. "Well, you're right about one thing," she drawled sarcastically.

"About you not liking me?"

"Apparently I didn't make that clear enough ten years ago."

Sloan laughed shortly. "You have to be kidding. You're not really letting what happened ten years ago influence you today."

Maggie faced him with a belligerent stance. "And why wouldn't I? Have you done anything to alter my opinion? What did you do ten years ago when you were dating *my* friend? What did you do when I came to your house to discuss the lease?"

Sloan's gaze roamed her face. "I kissed you. I'd like to do it again. Right now. An apology would be a lie. Is that what you want from me, a lie?"

"I don't want anything from you! Nothing, except your getting those stinking animals off my land!"

"Which is the one thing I won't give you." A hint of a smile touched his lips. "Go out with me, Maggie. Forget about sheep and cows and your ranch and mine. Let's go out tonight and have a few beers and get to know each other."

She sucked in a sharp breath. "I don't believe this conversation!"

"Believe it. I liked you ten years ago and I still like you. Don't ask me why. You've done everything but—" Sloan glanced around and spotted a bucket of paint nearby "—dump a bucket of paint over my head, and I still like you."

"Don't tempt me," Maggie retorted, eyeing the same pail of paint. "Look, apparently you have nothing to do but stand around here and badger me. But I'm sure that even you can see there's enough work to keep Les and me busy for weeks, so I'd appreciate being allowed to do it."

Sloan hesitated, then grinned and touched the brim of his hat. "If there's one thing I can do, it's take a hint." His eyes darkened. "But I'll be back, Maggie."

"I'm sure you will, but please confine your intrusion on Holloway land to your sheep. I don't think there's anything in that lease that gives you the right to annoy me!"

"You know, that's the very reason I don't quite believe you and I are a complete failure, honey. I annoy you much too easily." Sloan walked off laughing, with Maggie staring after him, her expression a study in perplexity.

The appointment with the attorney went well on Tuesday, and on Wednesday Maggie attended the cattle auction. Everything was falling into place. The purchase agreement would be ready for her signature in a few days, and she'd bought a hundred head of prime Black Angus, limiting herself on this first buy to young steers and mature, impregnated heifers. By fall she could recover some of her outlay of cash by selling the steers. Three to four months would add substantial weight to the animals, and any additional cost in their care throughout the summer would be minimal. She should make a decent profit on the steers.

The heifers would drop their calves in February and March, increasing her herd by at least forty head. The auction had been costly, but she had months before she would have to buy an Angus bull, which would be a major expenditure. Maggie planned to attend other summer auctions also, and she'd made friends and visited with several Angus breeders from the area. All in all she felt like she'd made an exceptionally good start in the business.

On Wednesday evening she celebrated by cooking a steak on the patio barbecue, and after Les had eaten and ambled off to his own quarters, Maggie sat outside by herself for a long time. Her thoughts were mostly pleasant, touching on the ranch, its past, present and future. If her grandfather was still alive, he'd be applauding her efforts, she knew, and it gave her a warm sensation to feel so productive.

When the sun dropped below the distant, mountainous horizon, Maggie got up and went inside. She quickly tidied the kitchen, then went upstairs for a shower and a little reading in bed. While she stood under the spray of water in the shower stall, though, the herd of sheep in her main pasture battered her mind again. She'd been trying very hard not to dwell on something she couldn't change, but at odd moments the image of Sloan's sheep eating her grass and drinking her water would strike her so hard, she'd get weak.

Maggie fought against resenting her father for the situation. She told herself he'd had the legal right to do whatever he'd wanted to with the ranch, even if he'd deliberately ignored family tradition. She even tried to tell herself it was time to put aside that old antagonism between sheep and cattle people. Like her grandfather, she had no other prejudices, and in every other aspect of life she despised bigotry. But disdaining sheep was almost as much a part of her as the color of her eyes.

Cattlemen passionately believed that sheep ruined grassland. Maggie remembered her grandfather talking about the little critters yanking the grass up by its roots, rather than biting it off like cattle did. "They kill the grass," Lyle Holloway had declared many times. "That's why sheepmen keep moving their herds!"

Whether or not that was true wasn't the real issue with Maggie. Her feelings were so deeply rooted, so ingrained by a man she'd adored and followed and emulated, that they weren't something she could wash away with the lather from her shampoo.

In all honesty, she wished she could.

After toweling off, Maggie went through her normal aftershower ritual, working body lotion into her skin, drying her hair, applying a moisturizer to her face. Then she pulled a pink cotton nightgown over her head and started for her bedroom. At that moment a startling idea struck her, and instead of snuggling down in bed with the book lying on the nightstand, she raced from the bedroom and down the stairs to the study.

With the grazing lease in hand, Maggie returned to her bedroom and climbed in bed. She reread the lease, slowly and thoroughly, and she finished the document with a satisfied smile. Nowhere, not in any of the clauses, was there any mention that the lessee had access to any particular portion of the lessor's land. Legally she could move Sloan's sheep to any pasture on the place. Her Angus were scheduled for delivery on Friday morning, and she wanted that main pasture for them. It had by far the best grass on the entire Holloway spread.

Maggie's pulse raced with excitement. Sloan would be furious.

But what could he really do, other than yell and try to intimidate her with masculine rage?

She'd given him fair warning that night at his house, and several times since, as a matter of fact, that she wasn't going to take his stubbornness without fighting back. Moving his sheep would be a positive statement, letting him know that this was her land and that she was adamantly opposed to the judgment her father had made on the matter. Sloan had said there just wasn't another place he could move his herd to, but Maggie had trouble believing that. It made a lot more sense to her that Sloan had preferred taking a stand on the lease.

This was her stand, or it would be. She would enlist Les's help in the morning and move that disgusting herd of smelly wool to the most distant pasture on the ranch. And if Sloan didn't like it, tough!

"Maggie, are you sure moving Prescott's sheep with no warning is a good idea?" Les was saddling his horse in slow motion, visibly reluctant to take part in the sheep drive.

Maggie snorted derisively and proficiently tightened Rebel's cinch belt. "Frankly I hope he gets so mad about it he hauls his damned sheep back to Wyoming where they belong."

"Well, he seems like a pretty nice fellow. Just seems a little underhanded to move his herd without telling him in advance."

Maggie raised an eyebrow. "I need that main pasture, Les. Why Dad ever let Sloan put his animals there in the first place is beyond me. It has the best grass on the whole place. Or, it used to," she added grimly.

"I guess your dad figured he wasn't using it, so someone might as well get some good out of it."

Maggie slapped the stirrup down into place. "Prescott's all through getting the 'good' out of this place. I can't run his sheep clear off the ranch, but I can get them out of sight." She swung up into the saddle and leaned forward to pat Rebel's graceful neck. "Good boy," she crooned.

Excitement kept Maggie lively during the ride to the sheep's present pasture. She had a coil of rope wound around her saddlehorn, as did Les, and she was wearing her boots and hat. She'd awakened positive that making even this reasonably peaceful move on the sheep was the right thing to do. When her Angus arrived tomorrow morning, they'd have acres and acres to themselves, and at the same time Sloan would get the message that Maggie Holloway still detested sheep.

For the next few hours Maggie had fun, plain and simple. Hazing the sheep into a moving sea of wool, and then anticipating the smelly little critters' dives for freedom from the pack and turning them back was fun. Of course, she'd never driven sheep before, although she'd done this sort of thing many times in the past with a herd of cattle. The sheep were a little quicker than cattle, and they also did some mighty strange things. Like bunching up and jumping over one another. Maggie found herself giggling over their antics, and caught Les laughing a couple of times, too.

Rebel wasn't really a cow pony, or in this case, a sheep pony, but he performed like a champ, stopping on a dime, spinning around, leaping to a quick run when necessary.

They were all tired when the sheep were finally secured in the back pasture, and headed back to ranch headquarters at a walk.

"What're you gonna tell Prescott when he learns he can't get to that back pasture in his pickup, Maggie?"

She shrugged. "He can borrow a horse, if he wants one, or he can bring his own. I really don't care how he takes it, Les."

Which was true. But by the end of the day with still no sign of Sloan, Maggie had to admit she'd been watching for him with a considerable amount of tension. It seemed a rather strange coincidence to her that the day she'd chosen to more or less declare war was one of the few that Sloan hadn't come by. She had no choice but to go to bed with that fretful knot of apprehension in her stomach.

Maggie walked around the compound the next morning, determining what job to tackle next. Other than the barn and house, which were both major projects, all of the exteriors of the outbuildings had been repaired and several of them gleamed with a new coat of paint. The corrals were sturdy again, the weeds were completely gone and the immediate fencing had been tautened, with new posts replacing the ones that had rotted away.

She was debating whether to begin painting another building or ride fencelines as her next project. Every foot of fencing on the place needed inspection, and because of the high cost of new posts and wire, Maggie wanted to do the job herself. It was often a matter of judgment whether a post needed to be replaced or merely braced, and she wanted to keep the cost as low as possible so she could use her money for more stock.

Les's hammer blows rang from inside the barn, where Maggie had put him to work reinforcing stalls. She was watching for the trucks that would be delivering her Angus, but once they'd unloaded the cattle into the main pasture, she would be free to get to work again.

Frowning slightly, wondering what time of day Sloan would make an appearance—after missing yesterday, he was bound to show up today—Maggie wandered over to the fence of the pasture where she'd moved the horses so they would be closer in. She whistled for Rebel, and the big horse pricked up his ears, nickered softly and came running over to the fence.

This was a genuine love affair, Maggie readily admitted as she petted and patted Rebel's nose and beautifully arching neck. The stallion was four years old, and Maggie had bought him as a colt and trained him herself. Despite his name, he was a big love, as gentle as a kitten. He serviced the handful of mares on the place, but none of them was a match, in bloodline or beauty, for Rebel.

For a moment Maggie stopped quite still, giving her pet a long, speculative look. "Yes, why not?" she finally said softly. Why not locate and buy a few mares of Rebel's caliber? They would be outrageously expensive: Rebel had been. But their foals would have unlimited possibilities of beauty and speed. Maggie had never raced Rebel, or even trained him for the track. But the big stallion ran like the wind, and some of his ancestors had been notable race winners. With the right mares, his offspring could make more money for the ranch than cattle ever could.

She didn't have enough extra cash to go into Thoroughbred breeding in a big way, but she was willing to start small and expand gradually. The idea was breathtaking.

The rumble of diesel engines snapped Maggie's head around. Three large trucks were approaching. The Angus were arriving! "Les!" she shouted. "They're here!"

One by one the truckers backed up to a ramp and unloaded their cargo. The cattle bellowed and bawled while being prodded from the trucks, but then, as unconcerned as you please, the moment the big black animals entered their new pasture, they dipped their muzzles into the lush grass and started eating.

Maggie leaned on a fence post and watched the process, with pride of ownership and a wonderful sense of satisfaction, while Les gave the truckers a hand.

"Well now, what have we here?"

Maggie whirled to face Sloan. His rock-hard expression was in profile, though; he was looking across the fence. "Handsome beeves."

"Yes," she agreed quickly, her heart suddenly in her throat. There was tension in his stance but it was controlled, and her brave words yesterday about not caring how Sloan might take her moving his sheep returned to taunt her. Warily she watched Sloan's hand come up and rub his jaw, as if he was deeply involved in figuring something out.

He spoke with exaggerated perplexity. "There's something different...."

Maggie tensed, but made no comment about his little charade. She sensed his anger, and prepared herself for what was coming by telling herself again that this was *her* land and she had every right to do what she did. But when icy blue eyes slowly turned her way, she had to forcibly stop herself from backing away.

"Where are my sheep, Maggie?"

His voice had been honey-smooth, but that's where the likeness to anything even remotely sugary stopped. If she was to rely entirely on Sloan's body language, she should be running for her life. His tall frame reeked of fury, from the crown of his black Stetson to the pointed toes of his dusty black cowboy boots. Everything in between, the white shirt and jeans as taut as the body they covered, fairly exuded cold rage.

She cleared her throat. She'd expected this, and just because its reality was a little more daunting than she'd visualized was no reason to quake in her own dusty cowboy boots. Gathering the courage that seemed traitorously bent on deserting her, Maggie raised her chin. "I moved them."

Sloan's eyes bored into hers. The noise of the truckers and Les finishing up, the clatter of racks and ramps being put away, the slam of steel trailer doors, some masculine laughter and wisecracking, dimmed in the strength of the look Sloan was giving her. "*You* moved them? By whose authority?"

"Miss Holloway?"

One of the truckers was walking over, and Maggie tore her gaze from Sloan's. "Yes?"

The man held out a clipboard. "I need your signature on the delivery receipt."

"Yes, of course." Quickly Maggie scrawled her signature and handed the clipboard back to the trucker. He tore off a copy of the receipt, gave it to her and walked away.

The interruption hadn't alleviated Sloan's tension one iota, Maggie realized when she looked at him again. But it had helped her aplomb immensely. "There's only one authority on this ranch at the present, me," she said coolly.

"And you think that gives you the right to ignore a legal document and tamper with *my* animals?"

Maggie scoffed. "I didn't *tamper* with your animals, I *moved* them. And I didn't ignore the lease, either. For your information, I studied it very carefully, and there's not so much as a hint in it as to which Holloway grass your nasty little beasts have a right to graze on." Her eyes contained triumph. "I can move your herd anywhere I choose to, as long as it's still on Holloway land."

Sloan looked across the fence at the Angus, his jaw clenched, his expression hard. "You don't need this big pasture for your small herd."

"We both know this is the best one. I'm sure Dad gave you your pick of fields, and anyone with a lick of ranching sense can see that this is bottom land and subirrigated. It's got great grass, thick and dense and rich with moisture and nutrients. It's a beautiful field, but look at it just a little closer." Maggie pointed a forefinger across the fence. "Do you see the bare spot by that big rock? And those others along the creek? Your sheep were destroying this pasture."

Sloan's head snapped around. "That's a crock. Any bare spots out there now were there when the herd came in."

"Inasmuch as I wasn't around on that eventful day, I can hardly debate the point," Maggie retorted with a sniff, then glanced back over her shoulder. The cattle trucks' diesel engines were rattling to life, and Les was walking toward her and Sloan.

The hired man grinned weakly at Sloan, then asked Maggie, "Should I go on back, or hang around here?" With the big trucks lumbering away, two vehicles remained, Les's old pickup and Sloan's. Maggie had ridden out to the pasture with Les, and as the man was becoming accustomed to doing, he was awaiting her directive.

She was about to ask Les to wait a few minutes, positive she and Sloan could finish up quickly on the subject of moving his sheep, when Sloan intruded. "Go on back, Les. I'll bring Maggie. We still have a few matters to discuss."

His tone wasn't one that invited argument, Maggie noted with a slight frown. She had no idea what else Sloan wanted to discuss, but she wasn't about to put Les in the middle of it. The poor man was already uncomfortable in Sloan's presence, all too guilty for his part in moving the sheep. "It's all right, Les. Go on back. I'll ride with Sloan."

"Sure thing."

Les's departure was rather eager, Maggie noted. She turned back to the fence for another shot of self-satisfaction from the sturdy black cattle grazing as contentedly as if this had always been their home. The herd was only a hundred head today, but in her mind's eye Maggie was able to multiply it by ten, by twenty. Someday, the Holloway ranch would boast thousands of Angus. Someday. She wasn't impatient, not with a labor of love. Black Angus cattle and

Thoroughbred horses. Maggie's heart beat faster just thinking about it.

"All right, let's get this settled."

Maggie turned and gave Sloan a cautious look. "Get what settled?" The only thing she had left to tell Sloan was which pasture his sheep were in now. Oh, yes, there was one more thing, wasn't there? He was no longer going to be able to reach his herd in his pickup, and passing on that information might be a bit sticky. But there really wasn't one sound reason why he should insist on checking on his sheep every day, and it wouldn't hurt him a bit to ride a horse out to that back pasture once or twice a week.

His eyes were leveled on her in a very disgruntled stare, and while Maggie couldn't help a rather female pang at so much male anger, she really didn't know the half of it. Sloan was furious and having trouble containing it. Maggie's superior attitude was intolerable. It wasn't what she'd said that had fed his fury, it was the way she'd said it. She'd talked down to him, as if her upper hand was so secure, there wasn't a snowball's chance in hell of him doing anything about her gall.

Bert Holloway had given him free rein. "Put your sheep wherever you want to, Sloan," he'd said. "My little herds of cattle and horses are fine any place on the ranch."

Only, Bert wasn't here now, and his daughter had other ideas. And those snapping black eyes and pouty, kissable lips camouflaged a tendency towards unscrupulous, unethical, unprincipled behavior. Maggie's goal, bringing the Holloway ranch back to its former level of success, was admirable, but she definitely needed a lesson in good sportsmanship.

Sloan purposely altered his expression, from angry, stern disapproval to unaccusing sobriety. "You're really planning on going into the cattle business full bore, aren't you?"

The comment had been made almost nonchalantly, and the abrupt change of pace took Maggie aback. "Why...yes."

"It's a rough row to hoe."

She was suspicious of his concern. "Because I'm a woman?"

"Not only because you're a woman, but that'll probably make it a little tougher. You should probably diversify."

Maggie's smirk wasn't very polite. "With sheep?"

"No," Sloan drawled after a reflective pause. "I don't think you could make it with sheep."

Her eyes widened. "You don't think I can make it with anything, do you?" With grim determination, she promised, "I'll make it."

"Well, that remains to be seen. Where can I reach your dad?"

Maggie colored at the implication that she wasn't in control here. Apparently Sloan didn't believe she was the authority she'd proclaimed. "What do you plan to do?" she said angrily. "Tattle? I happen to be in the process of buying the ranch. For all intents and purposes, I own the place right now."

"Well, that's wonderful for you, I'm sure. But my lease was signed by Robert Holloway, and I intend to talk to him about it."

"It won't do you one bit of good!"

"Won't it? I'm not so sure. But if you are, then you won't mind giving me a telephone number for him, will you?"

Maggie glared daggers at him. "You're an insufferable man."

"I'm an angry man, Maggie. And I'll tell you something else. If you were a man and had moved my sheep the way you did, this conversation wouldn't be quite so polite."

"Please don't do me any favors," she returned hotly. "A concession from a damned sheepman is the last thing I need."

"Get me the telephone number," Sloan said low.

"Gladly! Maybe when you hear it from Dad, you'll finally get the message!" She stormed off towards Sloan's pickup, stopped after a few steps and looked back. "It's at the house. Do you expect me to walk back and get it?"

Four

———

The silence in the cab of Sloan's pickup during the short drive was as thick as heavy fog. He had barely braked to a stop before Maggie jumped out and stalked to the back of the house. She despised having to prove her position here, especially to Sloan, and was mad enough to spit.

Maggie was stumbling through the back door before she realized Sloan was right behind her, but the dirty look she threw him didn't prevent him from following her to the study.

Plopping down at the desk, Maggie began shuffling through the litter of papers concealing its mahogany surface. This was another chore she had to get to, she thought irately. She'd been wondering just what Les had done to occupy his days before she'd started organizing his time, but now the question included Bert Holloway. Sarah kept house, cooked, and bowed and scraped at her husband's command, and was excused from any negligence as far as the ranch and paperwork went, simply because those things were completely beyond her ken. But, dammit, Bert could have at least kept his desk in order.

And *she*—Maggie—shouldn't have dropped that little piece of paper with her parents' recent array of telephone numbers in the midst of this mess!

"Here it is," she finally exclaimed, and quickly jotted down several numbers on another piece of notepaper.

Sloan had been leaning against the door frame, his arms folded across his chest. He came forward as Maggie stood up, and they both reached over the desk to pass the paper.

"Thank you. Now, I'd like to take a look at my sheep, if you'd be good enough to tell me how to locate them."

"They're perfectly all right."

"Would you even know if they weren't?"

Maggie flushed, with anger, with a suddenly palpitating heart. "I can assure you—"

"Assure and be damned! I'll reach my own conclusion, thank you very much."

This was disturbingly different than Maggie had visualized. She'd known that Sloan wouldn't be thrilled, of course. She'd even expected that he'd be ticked off. But in the end she'd anticipated him accepting that she'd operate the ranch to her personal satisfaction. Instead, he was defying her authority and had even gone so far as to ridicule her plans. And she still had to tell him he could only reach his sheep on horseback.

The courage that had been slipping and sliding in and out of her system suddenly seemed ten miles away. "Uh…you'll need a horse."

"A horse," Sloan echoed tonelessly, then exploded. "Of all the cheap, underhanded tricks, this takes the cake! If you wanted my sheep moved, you could have called me. And don't tell me there aren't other pastures on this place with roads. I know better! You deliberately stuck my herd in the most out-of-the-way spot you could find, didn't you?"

His anger, at last out in the open, fired Maggie's. It felt good to finally let go, to let him see just how deeply their conflict really went. "Read the lease you signed, Prescott! I can put your stinking sheep anywhere I want!"

"What about ethics? Don't you have any?"

"Maybe my ethics went down the drain when you wouldn't even give me the courtesy of taking me seriously the night I came to your house to beg you to let me out of that lease!"

"I couldn't tear up the lease! I told you that."

"I don't believe you couldn't have found another place for those sheep. Let me put it this way. If my dad had asked, would you have been so mule-headed?"

Sloan was leaning, palms down, across the desk. They'd been shouting, both so angry even the air was turbulent. They were nose to nose, the heat of each other's emotions a palpable force in the room. "Get off my ranch," Maggie hissed. "I might have to put up with your disgusting sheep, but I don't have to put up with you!"

"That's where you're wrong, sweetheart. Grazing rights give me access to my animals any damned time I want it."

"I despise you!"

"Now that sounds just like a female," Sloan taunted. "When does the name-calling start, honey?"

Shrieking in blind rage, Maggie's right hand leaped up, aimed for his insolent face. She'd never struck a man before, never had even felt an *urge* to strike a man before. But he'd provoked her to violence, and she wanted to wipe that smirk off his face so badly, she ached.

Sloan caught her wrist deftly, just an instant before her hand made contact with his cheek. "Just remember who started this," he muttered, and yanked her around the desk with the intention of paddling her behind. But the second she cleared the desk, she came at him again, fighting like a little wildcat.

"What the...?" She wasn't very big, but she was wiry and quick, and the only way Sloan could finally subdue her was to lock his arms around her and pin hers to her sides in the process. What came next wasn't planned. But she was up against him, breathing hard, and the femaleness he'd so recently denigrated was on full throttle. Her firm little breasts were scorching his chest, and she smelled like a woman. He just stopped thinking and kissed her.

Maggie growled her fury deep in her throat, but she was held too tightly to get away. And then all kinds of crazy things began to happen. Her blood began racing through her veins, and the heat of the anger she'd been suffering had been nothing compared to the meltdown she was undergoing in the pit of her stomach now. Strange little aches were developing in a very personal part of her body, and as if they had a mind of their own, her lips actually got softer and parted.

For his tongue, she admitted dazedly when she felt it, and then took it and finally savored it. Somewhere in the past few seconds her eyes had closed, and in the darkness behind her eyelids, reality was being transformed by sensation. The man holding her was big and strong and utterly male, and if he knew nothing else in this crazy, mixed-up world, he knew how to kiss.

She felt his chest, his thighs, his most manly part, all pressed to some part of herself. If bones could liquefy, she would accuse hers of doing so, because as skeletal strength went, hers was deteriorating. Her alter egos, Professor Holloway, teacher and mentor, and plain Maggie Holloway, optimistic cattle rancher, were discovering a third personality, one with unrestrained sensuality. One that yearned and wanted, one that was responding to whatever magic this man was dishing out in such heavy doses.

Sloan's arms relented, and instead of slapping or scratching when hers were freed, Maggie lifted them to his neck. She felt a big hand push her hat off and thread through her hair. The air was still turbulent, but from an entirely different kind of passion, and when they both needed oxygen, it was taken in by only brief gasps between kisses.

There were sounds to such uninhibited lovemaking, Maggie realized dimly. Harsh breathing, the friction of clothing on clothing, soft, wordless vocalizations of pleasure. She heard a distant moan from herself, a rumbling growl from Sloan. His mouth lifted from hers, but he caught her bottom lip between his teeth, and then kissed her again, with increased hunger.

His hands began roaming, seemingly greedy, cupping her bottom one moment, rising to her back the next. She was fascinated with the way his hair whorled on the back of his neck, and just as he'd done with hers, she flicked his hat away. His hair was wonderfully resilient, thick and springy in her hands, warm and alive. His smell was familiar, of the outdoors, of leather and denim, and unique in something tangy and slightly spicy.

It wasn't until Sloan began unbuttoning her blouse that Maggie understood where this was really going. She should have known immediately, she realized, but then she'd never been swept away like this before.

She jerked her hands down and caught his, and then tilted her head back to break the kiss. "No. This is too much, too fast," she said in a voice so breathless and husky she hardly recognized it as her own.

"Maggie..." Sloan's head was swimming, but it wasn't his head that was urging him to try verbal persuasion. He was hard and aching, and right at the moment he wasn't quite able to grasp distinctly how much more he wanted Maggie Holloway than any other woman he'd ever known.

There was a big question in Maggie's mind about the confusion she was feeling. A few minutes ago they'd been screaming at one another, and the reasons for such outrageous behavior hadn't changed just because they'd ended a rather physical battle in each other's arms. The question was, how could she both hate and want a man?

Clearing her throat, Maggie tried to step back. But Sloan's hands had moved to her waist and were urging her to stay right where she was. "Maggie, I didn't mean for this to happen, but—"

"It changes nothing."

His gaze washed over her features, studying, probing, searching for something. "It changes a lot."

"Like what? Do you think a few kisses are suddenly going to make me like sheep?"

He openly winced. "Can't you forget sheep for a few minutes?"

Turning her head, Maggie looked away from the heat and the questions in Sloan's eyes. An odd embarrassment inhabited her brain. That old prejudice seemed foolish when narrowed down to specifics. Like Sloan had previously pointed out, this was a different age than the one her grandfather had lived in. She considered herself an enlightened woman, a modern woman, but one with a strong foundation of traditional beliefs. Her roots were deep and tenaciously planted, her ancestry worthy of pride. Above all else, though, she was a Montanan through and through, influenced from birth by a man whose death she still mourned.

Perhaps that was the heart of the passion that had burst to life at first sight of sheep on the ranch. Maybe her stand with Sloan was more a matter of loyalty to her grandfather's credo than a statement of personal preference.

Or, was she changing hats because of the big hands on her waist, the memory of hot, persuasive kisses on her lips and the masculine aura that was still making her knees weak?

She could relax her viewpoint only so much, maybe out of loyalty to her grandfather, but also out of loyalty to herself. "Sheep shouldn't be so important, should they? But then, maybe my plans for this place shouldn't be important, either. But they are. I've lived with a dream I didn't even realize I had until this summer. I want this ranch to become again what it once was.''

Maggie took Sloan's hands and lifted them away from her waist. Evading his attempt to lace their fingers together, she dropped his hands and moved away from him. She knew her face was flushed, and she could feel that her mouth was swollen. He'd kissed her hard and long and quite a few times, and Lord help her, she'd kissed him back the same way. There was no denying the sexual pull between them; it was too strong to bury her head in the sand and pretend it wasn't present.

But she wasn't a child. She was a thinking, mature woman, and she had the power and ability to say no when it made more sense than saying yes. Even to the demands of her own body.

"I'll loan you a horse if you want to ride out and check on your herd," she offered without looking at him, and it took a moment before she realized she wasn't getting a response on the matter. "Did you hear me?" she asked, turning to see his reaction.

He was staring at her, and for just a second, just before he blinked and rearranged his expression, Maggie thought she got a glimpse of little-boy hurting in his eyes. It was there and gone so fast she doubted her interpretation, especially when Sloan said rather brusquely, "I heard you. No, thanks. I'll come back tomorrow."

"Suit yourself," she said softly.

Sloan bent over, snagged his hat and then stood holding it. He was deeply unsettled over their almost savage embrace and kisses, and Maggie looked rather unfazed over the whole thing. She hadn't been, he knew. She'd kissed and groped as wildly as he had. True, she'd put a stop to it when he would have gone on and on. But she'd wanted exactly what he had. What he still did. It was an emotional blow to realize she was going to keep that old fence separating sheep and cattle people unbreachable.

Desire and a strange, dull ache in his heart brought Sloan across the room. He wanted to touch Maggie one more time before he left. He saw a flash of wariness enter her eyes when he drew near to her, but she didn't flinch when he got close enough to gently finger her hair. "I don't understand all of this, Maggie. Do you?"

Maggie steeled herself against too much feeling. "It seems pretty... basic to me."

"Basic? Yeah, I guess it is pretty basic. You're a flame, Maggie. I felt it ten years ago and I still feel it. But I guess you're right about it not changing anything."

"You don't like cattle any more than I like sheep, do you?"

He found a weak grin. "My family has raised sheep for over a hundred years. Our ancestors probably took potshots at one another."

She had to smile, but before she could say anything, Sloan did. "You know that I was married once, don't you?" Startled, Maggie's smile faded. "I've been divorced for three years now."

What did he want her to say? Maggie asked herself. His personal life, especially his past personal life, was none of her business. "Should I be empathetic?" she questioned quietly.

"No. Nor sympathetic. I just wanted you to know."

"Why? What just happened is not going to happen again."

His gaze traveled her face. "Maybe I'm not as sure of that as you seem to be." He paused, then added, "On the other hand, with that lease between us, maybe there's no chance for anything else."

A sinking sensation in Maggie's stomach gave her a start. She swallowed a very suspect and sudden lump in her throat, but finally managed to heartily agree. "With that lease between us, there's no *room* for anything else."

"Possibly." Sloan walked away, then stopped at the door and settled his hat on his head. "I guess we both have to do what we think best, right?"

"That's the way I see it." Maggie frowned when Sloan fished the slip of paper with the telephone numbers out of his shirt pocket and crumpled it into a small wad.

"I won't need this after all. I know what I have to do, and calling your dad isn't it. See you tomorrow, Maggie."

What was he up to now? Maggie advanced three anxious steps in Sloan's direction. "What are you planning?"

A bit of a grin played with his mouth. "Nothing much. Just something I think best. See you, Maggie."

When Sloan was gone, Maggie directed her shaky legs to carry her back to the desk chair. She sat down, still staring at the door. *Just something I think best.* Damn! It had to do with the sheep, that's the one point she didn't have to speculate about. But what could he do?

He'd already done enough, Maggie thought resentfully. She certainly didn't need a potentially time-consuming relationship right now. She wasn't looking for romance or an affair or whatever the heck this emotional upheaval might evolve into with a little nurturing, and she simply was not going to tolerate it. The next time Sloan made a fast move, he was going to get an earful.

Slapping her palms down on the desk, rearranging several loose papers by the breeze, Maggie got to her feet. She'd find out what Sloan had in his bag of tricks in the morning, and sitting around unilaterally deciding to remain personally uninvolved was only wasting time.

After retrieving her hat, Maggie strode from the study and through the house. By the time she'd cleared the backyard, she had decided to saddle Rebel and inspect some of the ranch's outer fences. Getting away by herself, even for that dreary job, looked inviting now.

And she felt well within her rights to blame Sloan Prescott for that unusual hankering, too.

Rising early was a lifelong habit for Maggie. It was a rare morning when she slept past seven, and more normally she was stirring around well before six. That morning her first glance at the bedside clock caused a painful grimace: it was ten after four.

"Ridiculous," she muttered, and punched her pillow into a new shape. Actually she hadn't slept very soundly all night and had punched that pillow several different times. The truth was, yesterday's events lay like a dead weight in her stomach. *What can Sloan possibly do about his sheep?* had mingled most of the night, without the slightest consideration for Maggie's need of sleep, with *Why did I kiss him back?*

The light in the room gradually permitted Maggie to count the cracks in the ceiling, and she knew it was no use; she wasn't going to go back to sleep. Sighing, she stopped trying and threw back the covers.

The early morning was cool, as it always was, and Maggie slipped into a warm velour robe and brocade house slippers. On the way downstairs she smoothed down her hair, and in the kitchen she yawned and prepared the automatic drip coffeepot and switched it on. Then she went to the window, folded her arms and watched the pearly light of dawn take on a golden glow as the sun peeked over the rim of distant mountains.

Upright and reasonably alert, Maggie took another look at yesterday. She was weary of tearing it apart, but it wasn't possible to forget those moments in Sloan's arms. He'd made some serious inroads into her subconscious, into that personal and private part of herself that she'd never had any trouble controlling before. What kind of label did one put on the emotional turmoil Sloan was causing her?

Even if she made it very clear to him that she wouldn't put up with another pass, would she be able to forget the way he made her feel? Ten years ago he'd done the same thing, kissed her breathless. But she'd been young and full of spirited plans, anxious to go to college, eager to get her teaching career off the ground. Life had been too full to dwell on one toe-curling kiss from a man she couldn't like in any case.

But things were different now. She still had a lot of plans, but Sloan had managed to worm his way into them. He was a part of what was going on now, and would be, because of his damned sheep, throughout the summer. And yesterday's kisses hadn't been those of a hot-blooded youth. They'd been from a hot-blooded man, and everything female in her had responded and ached for more.

Sighing again, Maggie brought her eyes from the window to the coffeepot. It was in the final throes of its process, and she got a mug from a cabinet in anticipation of a cup of hot strong coffee.

But the distant yet unmistakable sound of a vehicle on the ranch's driveway diverted her. Maggie set the mug down and hurried through the house to a front window. She chewed her lip and frowned at the sight of Sloan's pickup, pulling a good-sized horse trailer, raising dust on the driveway.

He was back, very early and bringing his own horse, apparently. Clouds of suspicion held her in place for a few moments, then Maggie raced from the room and took the stairs at a dead run. Tearing her nightclothes off, she yanked on jeans, a yellow T-shirt, socks and boots in record time. She could hear the pickup arriving, then the silence of a deadened engine. A door slammed. *Another* door slammed, and Maggie stiffened, wondering who Sloan had brought with him.

Grabbing her hat, she dashed back downstairs, through the house and out the back door. Her speed stalled somewhat when she saw Sloan and another man unloading two saddled horses from the trailer.

She still didn't know his game, but she was immediately wary and approached the activity with a cautious expression. Sloan saw her coming. "Good morning, Maggie."

"Good morning," she mumbled, shooting a questioning look to the other man.

"Maggie Holloway, Chet Collins."

Maggie nodded at Chet, Chet smiled at her and Sloan grinned at both of them. "Chet works for me. He's going to help me this morning."

"Help you do what?"

"Move my sheep," Sloan stated calmly.

Maggie's stomach began knotting. She knew he wasn't talking about taking the herd off the ranch. "Move them where?"

"Back to where they belong. Back to the pasture I leased."

Maggie's mouth went dry. "Need I remind you—?"

"That the lease doesn't designate any particular pasture? No, you needn't spell that out again. But that omission works as well for me as you think it does for you. You see, when Bert let me put my sheep in his main pasture initially, it sort of set the rules. As I see it, anyway. Besides, there's more than enough space, grass and water for my herd and your cattle."

There had been very few times in Maggie's life when speech had been all but impossible. She'd been talking for a living, after all. Speech was a teacher's most elemental tool. Through tone and words, she could make a lesson exciting or dull, and Maggie had never had much trouble holding a class's interest. But right at that moment, with Sloan so confident he'd gained the upper hand, she was quite speechless.

She looked from Sloan's patronizing expression to the amusement on Chet Collins's face, and when her gaze flashed back to Sloan, she realized that he was getting a big bang out of besting her.

Yesterday's anger was only a tempest in a teapot compared to the fury suddenly raging through her system. "You're insufferable," she whispered hoarsely. He'd known yesterday he was going to do this, and she had stewed and worried about his intentions all night. She couldn't physically stop him from moving the herd again, but this was still her ranch. "I'll move them again the minute you leave," she threatened with a glare.

All trace of levity vanished from Sloan's face, and Chet Collins uneasily shifted his weight from one foot to the other in a movement that said quite obviously this wasn't so funny now. "No, you won't," Sloan said in a lethally quiet tone. "But if you try it, be prepared for the restraining order I'll have my attorney hit you with. You *will* live up to the terms of that lease, and you *will* leave my animals alone. And one thing more, Maggie. I'm a rancher first, but all the talent in the world for raising sheep or cattle or anything else isn't worth a snap of the fingers without a business head. This is business. Your attitude toward that lease isn't."

The color had drained from Maggie's face and her backbone seemed to have turned to ice. Sloan had put her neatly in her place, and she suddenly felt totally inadequate and on the verge of tears. She'd never before been backed into a corner like this, and the frustration of having no recourse was overwhelming.

She stole a shaky breath, uncertain as to what to do next, embarrassed to find herself so boxed in. Losing her temper would only make her look like a fool, a *bigger* fool than she already appeared to be.

And then she saw her only weapon, a flicker in Sloan's eyes, a softening, a relenting, *warmth!* He'd said his piece and was oh, so ready to put it all behind them. *He wanted her!*

Yes, of course. How could she have forgotten yesterday in the past few minutes? Or the night she went to his house? Or, as crazy as it seemed, what happened ten years ago?

A sense of balance returned to Maggie. Sometime in the very near future she was going to have the opportunity to do the same thing to Sloan that he'd just done to her, make him feel inadequate and overwhelmed. She wasn't ordinarily a vengeful person, but the image of putting him in *his* place, if only on a personal level, was too satisfying to question.

Her chin had risen. "Very well. I see that nothing I could say is going to change your mind. The fact that I own this place now means zilch to you, and the only thing you're concerned with is business. That's how you want it, that's what you'll get. Access to your animals does *not* mean access to my house, my barns, to any portion of this part of the ranch. Do you understand?"

Sloan's face took on a little color, but Maggie was certain she saw a determined light in his eyes. He was reading her opposition as another challenge, which she'd been almost positive he would do. She would have her chance to demean him as he'd just done to her, and while she might not have been able to win this battle of business wits, she'd bet anything he'd remember losing the next confrontation a lot longer than he'd remember his victory today!

"I understand," he said solemnly, and turned to Chet. "Let's go."

With her back very straight and her head very high, Maggie returned to the house. Then and only then, within the privacy of the downstairs bathroom, did she let the trembling she'd been fighting take over. But she absolutely refused to cry. Running cool water on her wrists, she also bathed her eyes and temples. Calmer, she went to the kitchen for that forgotten mug of coffee.

At the window again, she watched the two mounted men becoming smaller, less distinct, as they got farther away. Sloan's bright red shirt was much more visible than Chet's tan one, and Maggie's gaze stayed on it until men and horses disappeared over a small rise.

The episode had left more than the obvious wounds, she realized as she sat at the kitchen table. The sense of inadequacy Sloan's business logic had created was festering. She definitely knew how to raise cattle. She knew about the necessary state and federally required inoculations so the beeves would be salable for public consumption. She understood the advantages of proper feeding, the intricacies of good breeding practices, the possible trials of birthing and how to turn male calves into steers.

But as Sloan had so succinctly pointed out, ranching was a lot more than raising animals. Did she have a head for business? Perhaps that had been the underlying cause of Bert's failures.

Disturbed by that possibility, when Maggie saw Les stirring around outside she went out and suggested he stay busy painting that day. "I'm going to go through the ranch's books and records."

She spent the entire day examining every speck of paper in and on the desk and crammed into the oak file cabinet that was also in the study. Sorting and filing as she went, Maggie ended up that evening with two large plastic trash bags full of discarded paper.

When she finally went to bed, utterly exhausted, the study was neat as a pin, with everything filed in labeled folders in the oak cabinet and the ranch's books sitting on the desk, ready for inspection.

She would begin that task in the morning.

Five

──────

It didn't seem to bother the cattle and sheep to be sharing the pasture, Maggie noted from her perch on Rebel's back. Not that she'd thought it would. Cows and sheep were reasonably passive animals and exceptionally dull-witted, besides. They ate, drank, slept and mated, surviving on instinct alone. Aside from those similarities, however, Maggie saw a certain beauty in the sleek black hides of the Angus, while the sight of the sheep raised her hackles.

Maggie had deliberately ridden through that particular field. She could have moved her Angus to another pasture and worked at ignoring Sloan's sheep, but her spirit rebelled at the thought. Losing was one thing, but she had no intention of doing so meekly. Which Sloan was going to find out. One of these days.

It bothered Maggie that he hadn't shown his face for four days. For four days she'd anticipated the personal showdown she felt was inevitable, and each night she'd gone to bed frustrated. Then, probably because her mind was in such a turmoil, she'd had ridiculous dreams—with Sloan in the starring role—to contend with, some of them disturbingly erotic. She'd awakened several different times in the past four nights in a sweat, and the best cure for that bit of female foolishness, she felt, was a ride through the main pasture. Out there, among Sloan's bleating, nasty little animals, she was able to remember how he'd humiliated her that day in front of Chet Collins much more distinctly than she could in the middle of a dark night.

Clicking her tongue, Maggie urged Rebel forward. It was Sunday afternoon, a day that had begun with low-hanging clouds and a threat of rain. The air was warm and heavy with humidity, and Maggie felt perspiration between her shoulder blades and under her hatband. She'd gone to church that morning and had decided afterward to just relax and enjoy the rest of the day. Les had gone off somewhere, and after lunch Maggie had saddled Rebel for a ride.

Once away from the main pasture and its hundreds of wooly reminders, Sloan's irritating image retreated and Maggie was able to think of other things. The purchase agreement had been mailed to her parents and should be on its way back to George Shipley. For all intents and purposes, as she'd told Sloan, the ranch was already hers. But Maggie knew she'd feel much more secure once the document was signed by her and put into escrow. Which was what George had suggested. "We'll set it up with the Newley bank, Maggie. Then you can make your payments to the bank and they'll forward them on to Bert and Sarah. For a small fee they'll take care of computing the interest and principal and keep everything real businesslike."

Maggie had readily agreed. "Businesslike" made good sense to her.

She'd also begun a search for some Thoroughbred mares and had visited two ranches that raised Thoroughbreds. Neither had mares with the special qualities of Rebel, although she'd seen some pretty horseflesh. But Maggie was looking for the wonderful deep chest, long, arching neck, strong legs and that uniquely-shaped head of the classic Thoroughbred. Color was important, too, and bloodline.

The four days since that disturbing confrontation with Sloan hadn't been wasted. Another building had been painted and the ranch's books studied and finally understood. When that was accomplished, Maggie started a new set of records, one that would reflect only her ownership and transactions. She felt like she was truly on the right track, and the minute she received word from George that the purchase agreement was back in his possession, she was going to contact the university and cancel her teaching contract.

Maggie rubbed the back of her sweaty neck. She was far from the core of the ranch and could look back and see the buildings as miniatures in the distance. Then she looked ahead again and smiled. A grove of cottonwoods was in front of her, and in its midst was a pond. As a girl she'd often ridden out there on a hot summer day and skinny-dipped, and today looked like a perfect time to do it again.

When she reached the trees, Maggie looped Rebel's reins over a low branch, giving him enough length to reach the water for a drink. Then she undressed quickly, draped her clothes over the saddle and waded into the pond. Its bottom was hard and rocky and the water was no more than four feet at its deepest. But it was cool and satiny, and with a contented sigh Maggie laid back and floated.

She stayed for an hour, then dressed and rode back home.

Around six, the impending storm began to produce great rolling claps of thunder and piercing bolts of lightning. Maggie had broiled a small steak and made a salad for dinner, and she ate while reading the Sunday newspaper. The kitchen had grown so dusky from the storm that the ceiling light was on, but at a nearly deafening blast of lightning and thunder, the light flickered and went out.

"Oh, rats," Maggie muttered, and got up to try another light. Nothing worked; the power was out. She quickly assessed the situation. The power could be off all night; it had happened before. Which meant if she wanted to straighten the kitchen and have a shower before bed, she'd better get a move on while she could still see at all.

Washing the dishes took five minutes, then Maggie ran upstairs. The bathroom was even darker than the rest of the house because it only had one small window. But Maggie lit a candle, set it on the sink counter and hurried through a shower and shampoo. When she carried the candle into her bedroom, she heard the rain starting, beating the roof in a violent deluge.

She threw on a lightweight cotton robe and ran around closing windows on the second floor. Then she started downstairs, having remembered she'd left the kitchen window open against the sultry warmth of the pre-storm atmosphere.

The flash of headlights drew her attention, and she thought Les must have returned. But a minute later, when someone pounded on the back door, she had second thoughts. "Who is it?" she called.

"Sloan."

Maggie stopped dead in her tracks. Her hair was wet and unbrushed and her robe wasn't the prettiest she owned. But maybe, just maybe, this was the moment she'd been waiting for, the opportunity to strike Sloan Prescott the blow to his ego he so richly deserved.

"Open the door, Maggie! I'm getting drenched."

She'd brought the lighted candle downstairs with her, and setting it on the kitchen table, Maggie unlocked and opened the door. A gust of wind-driven rain struck her as Sloan hurried in. He took off his hat and wiped water off his face. "This is a dilly of a storm."

She couldn't keep the wryness out of her voice, no matter how hard she tried. "Some people have sense enough to stay in when it's raining this hard. What are you doing here in the dark?'' He couldn't pretend to have come to check on his sheep, not with the storm creating a premature nightfall.

The candlelight was completely inadequate, casting more shadows than doing any real good. Sloan stared, then wondered if she knew that he could see three dark smudges through her pale robe. He decided that no, she probably didn't know, and if it wasn't for the odd lighting in the room because of that candle, he wouldn't be getting such an arousing view.

Arousing was maybe too mild a word for the surging in his loins. ''I came to see you,'' he admitted bluntly.

Maggie leaned her hips against the counter. ''Haven't you been neglecting your precious sheep the last four days?''

''Have you been counting?''

She should open the door and send him packing, the insolent, conceited *sheeper!* ''No, I haven't been counting,'' she said sweetly. ''But you were so attentive to those little beasts, and then ignored them for four whole days. Do you think they managed to survive without your constant pampering?''

Sloan grinned. ''Aren't you curious about why I came to see you? Or would you rather argue about my sheep again?''

She folded her arms, blocking out two of those interesting smudges. ''All right, I'll bite. Why did you come to see me? Surely you know how I feel about you.''

Sloan dropped his hat on the table alongside the candle. ''No, I think that's the problem. I really don't know. You see, I keep remembering how wild you were in my arms that day in the study. I had to ask myself, is that how a woman behaves with a man she loathes? And of course, Maggie, the answer is no.''

''It's obvious that was a one-man conversation,'' Maggie said dryly. ''Why don't you try it with another party? You might learn a thing or two with another opinion.''

"Do you think so?" Amusement tinted Sloan's tone. "All right, how about if I ask you that question. Does a woman open her mouth and arms to a man that she loathes, Maggie?"

If he would have added legs to that list, Maggie couldn't have blushed any hotter. She was glad it was too dark for him to see the changing hues of her skin. And so far, she realized uneasily, she hadn't found the opening to put him in his place. She would, though. She'd seen him staring at her robe. Any minute now he'd try something. And she wasn't above egging him on.

"Actually, Sloan, you, like most men, live with the misapprehension that women can only respond physically to men they love. Nothing could be further from the truth. Women function no differently than men."

"Is that a fact? It's fascinating information, Maggie. Tell me more."

He was making fun of her, but he'd change his tune before this was over, she thought grimly. "I don't know about you, of course, but I don't see a whole lot wrong with uninvolved sex." Maggie had trouble suppressing a giggle over the sudden shocked look on his face. "What's wrong?" she asked in the most innocent voice she could drum up. "Surely you haven't been thinking that your kisses were something special to me. Oh, that's really quite funny." She laughed and saw him wet his lips with the tip of his tongue.

"You want me to believe that, don't you?" he asked in an oddly constrained voice.

"*Want* you to believe? Frankly, Sloan, I don't give a damn what you believe."

He stared as if she'd just sprouted horns, and then grabbed his hat and started for the door. Maggie realized that she'd succeeded in striking her blow and waited for the elation she'd expected. There was none, nothing in her at all except a ludicrous emptiness. And then she saw him stop abruptly, toss his hat again and come at her. Her eyes widened. "Don't—"

It was all she got out before she was yanked up against him. His hands held her head, her neck, her shoulders, all at the same time, an impossibility that was entirely possible, she realized dazedly. His eyes bored into hers for a second, then his face came down fast, and his mouth on hers was open and rough and devouring.

She was locked between him and the counter, and his hips ground the front of his jeans into her. Every ounce of fight drained out of her, every desire to best him and demean him and put him in his place. He was hot and demanding and growing hard, and her senses reeled with all of the dizziness of a speeding merry-go-round.

Her hands rose to his forearms, more to support herself than anything else, and she felt the dampness of his shirt and the hair on his skin where the rolled-up sleeves stopped. His breathing was as heavy as the storm outside, and then Maggie heard her own attempts to get air when her mouth was busy doing something else.

Oh, damn, she thought wildly, as uncontrollable desire built and spread and seemed to be burning her insides. She shouldn't have taunted him with lies, not when she knew that he took everything she said and did as a challenge. He'd started for the door, obviously shaken over her out-of-character remarks about taking sex lightly. She didn't, of course. But she'd wanted to shake him, she'd wanted him to think his kisses were nothing special.

Well, they were, and he was proving it very effectively.

Her knees were as limp as wet dishrags when he raised his head. "Nothing special?" he growled.

She swallowed. They were alone here, in a deepening darkness that was barely disturbed by that puny candlelight. And the fury of the storm was enough to make her hair stand on end, even if Sloan hadn't already succeeded in that particular endeavor. "I think you better leave," she whispered, having failed with a normal voice.

"Leave? No, not yet," he purred. "You don't mind un-involved sex, you said. And you're sure as hell all worked up, honey. It would be cruel for me to kiss you like that and then leave you hanging."

"Sloan..." She did her best to put a warning in his name, but if he heard it, he ignored it. He brought his face down again, but only caught her bottom lip between his teeth for a sexually charged moment. "You have the wrong idea," she moaned when he was only breathing hard on her mouth.

His lips teased the corners of her mouth, and his hands moved in her still damp hair. "Been out in the rain, too? Maybe neither of us has good sense."

"I just got out of the shower." Her voice was low and husky, breathy. She didn't know what to do with her hands, and left them where they were, clasped around his fore-arms.

"Hmm. That's why you smell like lavender. Or, is it li-lac?"

"It's neither. Sloan, you're squashing me against the counter."

"Am I now?" His hands slid down her back, blocking her behind from the cutting edge of the counter. "We don't want bruises in such a delicate spot, do we?" he said, brushing his lips over the smooth skin of her face, taking great delight in kneading that "delicate spot." "You've got a great . . . posterior, Maggie, my love."

His lips moved across her forehead, lingered at a temple, then drifted down her cheek to her mouth. Maggie closed her eyes, her mind a muddle of conflicting emotions. Outside, the sky lit up with a tremendous flash of lightning, and an immediate crack of thunder shook the house. The kiss became more intense, as if incited by nature's unleashed fury. Sloan caught Maggie's hands and brought them up to his neck, then locked his around her. He moved against her, a rhythmic, suggestive rocking, and his tongue probed the hot, wet interior of her mouth with the same rhythm.

Maggie had never experienced anything quite like the untamed, unrestrained behavior going on in her nearly dark kitchen. The candle was only a feeble flicker, but the room erupted into eerie light every few seconds with another flash of lightning, followed instantaneously by earsplitting explosions of thunder. In between, the din of rain pelting the house was almost as nerve shattering. The storm had been brewing all day, and it occurred to an exceedingly dizzy Maggie that it had reached its peak.

Like she wanted to do. Like every cell in her shaken and breathless body was demanding she do. She didn't want to talk, she didn't want to think; she knew she'd stop herself if she did either. So she conveyed her wild and reckless desire through her body, her lips, her fingertips. She groped for his hair and clutched handfuls of it, and he groaned and kissed her harder. She sucked on his tongue, and she thought he would lift her robe and take her on the spot.

He did lift her robe, but he stayed in his jeans, and she became nearly faint with a new level of desire when she felt his hands on her bare skin. They were on her back, on her buttocks, then squeezing between their straining bodies to find her breasts. He tormented her nipples, teasing them with tender caresses.

He deserved some teasing, too, she thought with a vague hope of showing him he wasn't the only one who could inflict torture with tenderness. There was little breathing time between kisses, only harsh gulps and gasps, and she had no opportunity to see what she was doing. Blindly she searched for the buttons on his shirt, and when she realized they were snaps, she jerked them open.

At the same time she felt her robe drooping, being pushed off her shoulders. Sloan released her lips, and she shook the robe free and concentrated on the vista of the bronzed and hair-covered chest an opportune bolt of lightning provided. "Maggie . . . you're beautiful, more beautiful than I dreamed," she heard Sloan say in a hoarse, raw voice.

But she was caught up in her own dream. Mesmerized by the masculine beauty before her, she ran her hands over his chest, tangling her fingers into the mat of hair between his nipples. She lost contact then, because he bent his head to kiss her breasts. His mouth opened around one swollen nipple, and his tongue swirled over it.

"Oh, Sloan," she whispered feverishly, lost in the grip of the most intense desire of her life.

"You want what I do."

"Yes," she breathed, unable to deny it. A flash of lightning lit the room again, and she realized that the candle had gone out and the lightning was all they had. She reached for his belt buckle with trembling hands and undid it.

"Don't stop now," he urged when she hesitated, and when she didn't go on, he took her hand and pressed it to the zipper of his fly. "Do it," he whispered.

She could feel hard male flesh behind the fabric, and had one sensible thought. "Do you have something with you?"

"Yes, don't worry."

Boldly, eagerly, she pinched the tiny zipper tab and slowly slid it down. Sloan let go of her then to shed his clothes. Maggie watched, standing naked in the lightning-silvered room, as his shirt, his boots and socks, his jeans and briefs landed in a heap on the floor.

Lightning crackled and thunder roared, and Sloan caught her by the arms and brought her down to the floor, too. He spread his jeans and his shirt out and laid her on them, stretching out beside her. His mouth sought hers immediately. "We don't have to use the floor," she whispered.

"I want to. I want you here, now."

His kiss was hot and stole her breath, demanding every ounce of her passion, everything female in her. "Touch me," he whispered. "Like this." His hand traveled down her stomach, to her thighs and in between. Her heart leaped into her throat at the rush of pleasure she felt.

"Like this?" Maggie trailed her fingernails down his hard belly to his hair-roughened thighs. But she didn't probe between them, as he was doing to her. She returned to his hardened manhood, pressing against her hip. "Or, like this?" she teased huskily, encircling him and beginning a slow stroke.

She felt a gasp rocket through his body. "Not too much of that, or this will be over before it really begins."

"What's too much? Shall I stop?"

"Oh, Maggie," he groaned, and took her lips hungrily. They kissed until they were both gasping, and while Maggie stopped stroking, Sloan didn't. She couldn't lie still, and her hips rose and fell, again and again. Somewhere in the back of her mind she realized his expertise, that he knew so very well what to do. But the thought was lost when the waves of incredible pleasure began, and she heard her own uncontrolled moans mingle with the cacophony of thunder and lightning.

He held her then, bringing her face to his chest, stroking her back, her hair. Maggie was dazed, stunned by the degree of emotion she'd just undergone. It took minutes for her breathing to subside to normal, and with it she began to think again.

It seemed utterly shocking that she was lying on the kitchen floor with Sloan, stark naked and making love. Had she completely lost her mind?

She felt him stir, and with movement she became all too aware of how aroused he was. His body was hard and hot against her, certainly not satisfied or fulfilled the way hers was. He had seen to her pleasure first, before his, a commendable generosity. Still, she was about to make some kind of protest against continuation of this shocking intimacy when his mouth captured hers in a kiss of utter possession, and strangely, her pulse fluttered like a crazy thing again.

His hands moved over her, caressing the hollow of her throat, her breasts, the indentation of her waist, the soft skin of her inner thighs. She was amazed to feel such desire again, to want him so much. Something deep within her body ached, a point of searing, demanding heat. It was a brand new sensation, something she'd never felt before, and she didn't object when he went into his wallet for a small foil-wrapped packet.

But she didn't want this to continue on the floor. And while he was sitting up, she got to her feet. "Upstairs," she said huskily. Maggie took his hand.

They made their way through the dark house, aided by lightning, although the storm was passing now. In her bedroom, Maggie led him to the bed, then dropped his hand to throw back the bedding. Then she laid down and drew him down on top of her. "Maggie," he whispered, and kissed her ardently.

Her hands moved on his sweat-slickened back and shoulders. She felt strangely in command, awash with desire, yet somehow understanding it. She'd thought she had long ago faced her own sexuality, but she knew now that her past experiences had been poor facsimiles of the real thing. That it was Sloan Prescott who had really awakened her was startling, but not intolerable, not when it was he who had given her the first adult kiss of her life ten years ago.

She felt his anguish, his need, and it fired her own, driving her to a restless writhing beneath his hands and mouth. She sensed a subtle shifting of power; hers diminishing, Sloan's intensifying. And finally, there was only mastery in his touch. He whispered in her ear, "Now, Maggie, now," and slid into the moist heated depths of her body.

Her breath caught, held and was released in a rush of renewed aching. He was hot and hard within her, reaching that secret place of unbearable heat. She raised her hips, asking that he extinguish the fire. And with that submissive movement, he took over completely.

The rhythm of his thrusts fogged Maggie's brain, for each inward plunge tantalized and created a need for another. She drew him deeper by lifting her hips and locking her legs around him. And the pressure grew, and grew, until she was weeping and clutching his back.

The explosion of her release blinded her and made the pleasure she'd achieved on the kitchen floor pitiful by comparison. Again and again, in surging waves, the most desirable of raptures made her cry out. Submerged in their glory, Maggie only vaguely heard Sloan's triumphant cry.

And then the bed was still. The air was still. And only their breathing broke the stillness.

Her first clear thought was that the storm was over. Even the rain had stopped.

Then her mind began working, and she closed her eyes and listened to the thumping of her heart. Her body was limp with the most incredible peace she'd ever experienced. But she thought of her flip remarks about uninvolved sex and gnawed her bottom lip with her sharp little teeth.

Sloan's head came up, and he rested on his forearms to see her. "Maggie, sweet Maggie," he said softly. "Would I sound smug if I said I knew it would be like that for us?"

Even in the dark she could see pinpoints of light in his eyes. The satisfaction in his voice oddly annoyed her, perhaps because it was how she felt, too, but she also knew what a disaster this really was. Uninvolved sex? The term was a contradiction in itself. There probably was no such thing, not unless the people were total strangers and never saw each other again after the fact.

Still, it wasn't a philosophy she intended debating with Sloan. She would, at least, lead him to believe she was emotionally unaffected. That she was deeply shaken and wondering how one continued with an ordinary life after such an extraordinary experience was really none of his business.

When she made no reply at all, Sloan sighed and moved away. "Which way's the bathroom?"

"To the left, first door down, also on the left. Try the light switch by the bedroom door on your way out. The storm is over. Maybe the power is on again."

It wasn't. The switch clicked lifelessly, and Sloan left feeling his way in the dark.

Maggie realized that in all honesty she didn't know what to do next. She'd never touched the stars so keenly before. What did one do after such a communion of mind, body and emotion? Wryly she even wondered if thanks were in order, if she should commend the man who'd stirred her to such a level of bliss.

The problem with the whole episode was that the man was Sloan Prescott. She didn't want to be involved with a sheepman. In further examination of her feelings, Maggie admitted she didn't want to be involved with *any* man right now, not with all of her plans for the ranch just getting a foothold. But it seemed particularly disloyal to herself that she'd faltered so blatantly with Sloan. He'd deserved outright rudeness, some kind of stinging revenge, and she'd ended up making love with him. It was mortifying.

She heard him coming back and tucked the sheet across her breasts and under each arm. His bare skin was a montage of shadows, some lighter than others. The hair on his chest was a black design, narrowing down his belly until it reached another solid black design at the top of his thighs. She couldn't stop looking. But she was having trouble breathing normally again. "It...it's very stuffy in here. Would you mind opening a window?" she asked.

He had been heading directly for the bed, and Maggie thought of jumping up before he finished with the window. But she knew that at some point she was going to have to face Sloan with the aftermath of her behavior. And facing him in the dark right now suddenly seemed easier and simpler than avoiding the issue until the lights came on.

With two windows open, a lovely cool breeze entered the room. The air was clean and damp and smelled so good, Maggie gulped it in with a thankful sigh. "Thank you."

Sloan approached the bed, and she could see the shadows of his body a little more distinctly. He was beautiful, she realized with a quickening breath, a pleasing example of rugged man.

But he was also overbearing, egotistical and completely coldhearted when it came to business.

And maybe when it came to women, too. He'd been awfully quick to jump on her stupid remarks about uninvolved sex, hadn't he?

The edge of the bed sagged with Sloan's weight, and he leaned over Maggie, bringing his face down to within a few inches of hers. "Ready to talk a little?" he asked quietly.

"Certainly," she bravely lied.

"You're nothing like my ex-wife."

"What?" she asked numbly, completely astounded.

"I just wanted you to know that. Once burned, a man tries to avoid the same kind of fire. I suppose women do that, too, after a bad marriage."

"I . . . would think so," Maggie agreed, without a whole lot of conviction. "I'm not sure I see your point."

"You don't? Well, I'm not explaining myself very well, I guess. Honey, this was special tonight. After this I sure can't see myself interested in other women."

Maggie's mouth dropped open. "Sloan...for God's sake, don't read more into it than . . ."

"Than what?" He began toying with her hair. "What we just shared wasn't uninvolved, Maggie. I feel plenty involved." He studied her. "Are you telling me you don't?"

She cleared her throat. "I haven't told you anything. You're the one who's done the talking. But I do have an opinion, if you want to hear it."

"Of course I want to hear it."

Maggie wished now that she'd gotten out of bed when she'd had the chance. She felt vulnerable and at a distinct disadvantage huddled under the sheet. And darkness or not, Sloan hadn't made even one stab at modesty. He could at least have wrapped a towel around his middle.

"All right. First, I won't pretend that tonight wasn't exciting. It was. But we're both adults, and—"

"Exciting? Is that what you said, exciting?"

"Yes. Is there something wrong with the word?"

"Exciting, but uninvolved, right?"

"Frankly, yes. Sloan, this shouldn't have happened. What does it change? Let's clarify that very quickly. Because of tonight are you going to come over in the morning and get your sheep out of my hair?" She felt him stiffen and then draw away from her. "See what I mean? It changed nothing, did it?"

"It *had, has* nothing to do with my sheep! Of all the illogical females, you take the cake!"

"Illogical? You're the one who's illogical. You're the one who wants to believe that an hour of passion just automatically eradicated all that tension and bickering between us. I'm logical enough to realize that it couldn't possibly. I'm still me, you're still you. Tomorrow morning, Sloan, you're going to wake up and still be a sheepman, and I'm going to wake up and go out and see my Angus. Then I'm going to go ahead with my plans for this ranch. Like I said, tonight changed nothing."

"Oh, good Lord," Sloan muttered, and got to his feet. "Maggie, you're enough to drive a man to drink. Where are my damned clothes?" He started for the door and drove his big toe into a bureau leg. He cursed loudly and efficiently, then limped to the doorway and vanished.

Maggie stared at the blackness that had just swallowed him up. He was out of sight, but she could hear him feeling his way down the stairs. He'd gotten the message, loud and clear. And yes, as foolish as she'd been, she could look at the culmination of the evening as the revenge she'd wanted.

Then, dammit, why did she feel like bawling?

Six

"I received the purchase agreement from your folks in today's mail, Maggie."

Maggie clutched the telephone and closed her eyes for an emotional moment. The ranch was hers, lock, stock and barrel. Or, as legally hers as it could be with years of payments ahead of her. That was okay, though. She didn't mind making payments to her parents one little bit. "Thank you, George. I'll be in this afternoon to sign it."

"Fine. I'll shoot it to escrow then, which will wrap the whole thing up."

Maggie noticed her erratic pulse beat as she set the phone down. The ranch was hers. There was only one more formality to see to, her signature on the agreement. It was happening—it was actually happening!

Excitement raced through Maggie's system. She'd been living in a state of nearly holding her breath, she realized. Bert and Sarah could have changed their minds, and that niggling thought had been impossible to completely ignore. But they hadn't. The ranch was hers!

Maggie wanted to tell someone how elated she was, but she'd sent Les to Newley for a load of fence posts and barbed wire. She thought of friends in Bozeman, but they'd scattered for the summer. And besides, their hearts were in teaching, unlike hers, which hadn't been able to get over a first love, the ranch. They would say how nice her good fortune was, but which of them would really understand?

Only another dedicated rancher would understand why she felt close to bursting with emotion. There were some she could have called, of course, neighbors, longtime acquaintances. But there really was no one special to share her good news with.

Except Sloan.

No. Sloan was *not* special! He wasn't. Sunday night shouldn't have happened. All she had to do was go outside and listen, to reinforce the animosity between them. The distant bleats of his sheep were evidence enough of where she and Sloan stood with each other.

Maggie had seen his black pickup twice since Sunday. But it hadn't come near the house, and she'd told herself both times how glad and relieved she was that Sloan was leaving her alone.

Walking through the house, Maggie heard Les's old pickup rattling in and she hurried out to meet him, putting Sloan aside again in the satisfaction of operating the ranch. *Her* ranch.

There was no hotter, harder work on a ranch than putting in new fence posts in July, Maggie thought, wiping the sweat off her face with the sleeve of her shirt. Les was stripped to the waist, which Maggie wished she could do, and the older man's skin had burned to a deep, dark mahogany. They'd been repairing fences for nearly a week, and they were still only about a third of the way through the maze of barbed wire and posts on the ranch.

Maggie was determined to see it through. Hiring another man to help Les would have been spending money she wanted for stock. The exciting part of that goal was that she'd found three beautiful mares and was in the process of negotiating a price with their owner. The only thing Maggie knew for sure was that the price was going to be high, and she didn't want to waste an unnecessary dollar on hiring extra help, not if she could do the work herself.

Still, the days of hard physical labor under a gruelling sun appeared to be a lot easier on Les than they were on her. It was amazing to Maggie that the older man seemed to be thriving, while she just seemed to lose a little more steam each day. She hadn't had the energy to take Rebel out for even a short jaunt since the fence project started, having been exhausted and eager for bed very early each night.

"Haven't seen much of Prescott lately," Les said when he stopped for a drink of cool water from the thermal jug they kept with them.

They were working on the south fence of the main pasture, and Maggie glanced at the groups of sheep and cattle they'd shooed away from that section of the wire. "No, he doesn't come around as much," she said quietly. "And when he does, he confines himself to this pasture. It's what I asked him to do, Les."

"Well, I know, but..."

Maggie walked away. She didn't want to discuss Sloan, not with anyone.

Two days later, on Friday evening, she was sitting on the back patio, rather listlessly watching the sun going down. Everything was going so well with the ranch that Maggie knew darned well her unrest had to do with Sloan; he and his wretched little animals were the only flies in her ointment. The big question was, however, which bothered her more: Sloan's previous and predictable intrusions on her life, or his present extended absence?

Maggie shook her head in complete disgust. Number one, she wanted those damned sheep out of her main pasture, and number two, she was glad, *glad*, that Sloan was staying away!

She was tired, that was her problem. And maybe just a little bit lonely. What she needed was a change of pace, maybe an evening out. An evening with music and jokes and lots and lots of laughs.

There was a place where she could find music and laughter, and it wasn't very far away, either. Shannon's Saloon and Dance Hall just outside of Newley. There were bound to be people she knew at Shannon's on a Friday night.

Why not? Maggie pushed herself out of the chair. Yes, why in heck not? If by chance everyone at Shannon's *was* a stranger, she didn't have to stay.

An hour later Maggie came out of the house ready to go. She was wearing perfume and makeup and a gorgeous yellow silk blouse with her tight jeans and high-heeled dress boots. The ends of her straight hair were turned under at her shoulders, which was about all the fussing she ever did with her glossy mane.

She was about to get into her car when she spotted Les at one of the corrals. "I'm going out, Les," she yelled.

"Okay, Maggie. Where to?"

"To Shannon's. See you in the morning."

"Have fun."

Maggie wasn't gone fifteen minutes when Sloan drove up. Les ambled over as Sloan got out of his pickup. "Evenin', Les. Maggie's car is gone."

"She left about ten, fifteen minutes ago, Sloan."

Sloan frowned. "Well, I guess I can discuss it with you. Maybe you already heard about it anyway."

Les leaned against the fender of Sloan's pickup. "Heard what?"

"About that dog pack running around wild. It brought down four sheep in the area in the past week. Seen any sign of wild dogs around here?"

"I sure haven't, Sloan. Never even heard about it, as a matter of fact. I'll tell Maggie."

"Well, they don't bother mature cattle or horses, which is all she has on the place. A sheep, though, isn't any match for a pack of hungry dogs."

"Nope, it ain't."

Sloan glanced at the empty parking place that Maggie's car was always parked in. "She went out, huh?"

"Yeah, she did."

When Les didn't volunteer anything, Sloan reached for the door handle on his pickup. "Well, guess I might as well be going. Tell Maggie about the dogs."

"I will. And I'll keep an eye out, Sloan. I'm still pretty good with a shotgun."

"Thanks. I'll be over more often to check on the herd, too." Sloan swung up onto the seat. "Is she with friends?"

"Maggie?" Les scratched his head. "Gosh, I don't know. She just said she was going to Shannon's."

"Oh, Shannon's. Great. Thanks, Les. See you tomorrow."

Maggie was in luck. When she walked into the old, barn-like structure that passed for a dance hall and saloon, she saw several people she could call friend. In minutes she was sitting at a table with a glass of cold beer in front of her. And laughing, too. It felt marvelous.

Because it was a Friday night the place was busy. A live band was due to start playing at nine, but people were wandering in early to get good tables, those closest to the dance floor. Maggie didn't intend a late night, not with she and Les planning an ordinary workday the next day. But it was wonderful to kid around with friends.

Numerous stops at her table consisted of inquiries about her folks, and Maggie responded to one and all that Bert and Sarah Holloway were having a great time campaigning.

Shannon's kept getting a little more crowded all the time, but it stunned Maggie to notice Sloan at the bar and realize that she hadn't seen him come in. From her position he was in profile, holding a beer, talking to two other men, one of whom Maggie recognized as a local cattle rancher with a small but successful operation. She was struck again, as she'd been at the church that first Sunday, that no one but her seemed to hold Sloan's preference for sheep against him.

Her gaze kept returning to him. Taller than his immediate companions, Maggie admitted again what a good-looking man he was. His body had a lean suppleness, his movements were smooth, sexy and masculinely graceful. Dressed like every other man in the room, in jeans and a western-cut shirt, he still stood out.

It wasn't just Sloan's looks that stirred her, though. There'd been too much between them to look at the man across a room and not remember. Between laughing comments with friends about inane topics befitting their surroundings, Maggie's insides unexpectedly rebelled at circumstance. What fate had decreed Margaret Holloway and Sloan Prescott be on opposite sides of *any* issue? Why had they met again at this particular slot in time? Any one of the past summers, when Sloan's sheep weren't on Holloway land, and when she had only been a visitor to the ranch, would have been a much more auspicious time for them to run into each other anew.

Maggie sipped from her glass and furtively studied the group at the bar. Did Sloan know she was here? If he saw her, would he come over and speak?

Bottom line—did she *want* him to come over?

Maggie uneasily squirmed on her chair. Just what exactly was wrong with her? She didn't want Sloan around, and then when he adhered to her wishes, she didn't like that, either. How did one explain such ambivalence?

The musicians finally arrived, and after tuning up, the band broke into a lively opening number. People swarmed to the dance floor, and Maggie found herself being tugged along by an old friend of her father's. It was nearly impossible to dance in the crush, but it was fun anyway, and when it was over she was escorted back to the table laughing and breathless. Darting a glance to the bar, Maggie saw that Sloan still seemed completely oblivious to her presence.

Then, one after another, most of the men she knew claimed a dance. During one slow number, Jake Barnett, another older friend, gave Maggie something to think about. He asked after Bert and Sarah, which Maggie had fully expected. She repeated the pat answer she'd given to at least a dozen others already tonight. "I talk to Mother and Dad every three or four days. They're doing very well, Jake. Dad seems to love politics."

Jake chuckled and shook his head. "It won't last, Maggie. You mark my words, young lady. One of these days Bert will get lonesome for the ranch and just skedaddle for home."

It was on the tip of Maggie's tongue to explain her ownership, but something stopped her. Apparently word hadn't gotten around, at least not to Jake, and she realized she wasn't comfortable with the idea of telling him the story. His opinion was alarming, though, and Maggie tried to correct it. "Dad says he never wants to live on the ranch again."

Jake threw back his head and roared. When he stopped laughing he winked at Maggie. "Don't hold your breath, honey. I probably know your dad better than you do. We go way back, you know. And I'll eat this here Stetson without salt if he doesn't show up before Labor Day."

When Jake delivered her back to the table, Maggie decided to go home. The flavor had definitely gone out of the evening. Deep inside of her sinking stomach was the worry that Jake Barnett was right. Based on Bert's track record, who wouldn't feel like Jake did? It gave Maggie the start of a tension headache to realize she'd already thought of Jake's theory, but just hadn't let it gain distinction. Jake, darn him, had made her face it. Just what would she do if her parents should suddenly show up from out of the blue and want the ranch back?

Oh, they wouldn't! They couldn't!

Well, legally they couldn't. But legal didn't always cut it in family matters.

Maggie picked up her purse and said good-night to those around her table. She knew she had to walk right past Sloan to reach the door, but as far as she knew he hadn't even looked her way. And with his complete indifference as evidence, Maggie decided that it probably wouldn't make the slightest difference to him if she should march on by without so much as a hello.

She still wasn't sure if he'd seen her when she was out the door and crossing the parking lot to her car, which gave her a strangely hollow feeling. She wouldn't dwell on it, she decided. If Sloan was ignoring her, it was only what she'd demanded.

"Maggie!"

She drew a quick breath and turned. Sloan had followed her out, apparently. "Yes?"

He walked up with that pantherlike stride of his. "Hi."

"Hello."

"Leaving pretty early, aren't you?"

"I only intended to stay a few hours."

He leaned against the trunk of her car. "I didn't ask you to dance because I didn't want to embarrass you."

Maggie stared at him, fully comprehending the dig she was getting. She'd been so adamant about not wanting to be seen with a sheepman, and her changing attitude on that old issue was still a private matter, nothing she'd mentioned to anyone. Still, Sloan's sarcasm galled. "How considerate," she drawled.

He grinned. "I'm a considerate fellow."

He was also a sexy fellow, and it startled the hell out of Maggie to realize that little spot of searing heat was back in her lower stomach. Remembering how effectively and pleasurably Sloan had alleviated the condition scorched her cheeks. She was going to have to give this some serious thought, she realized in the back of her mind. Just talking to a man shouldn't do this to a woman.

But they weren't just talking, were they? There were quite readable intimations in his eyes and in the way he moved. He was thinking of their lovemaking and he didn't have to put it in words for her to get the message.

"I've got to go," she said, putting a need for haste in her voice.

He didn't move away from her car. "I knew you were here. I stopped by your place and talked to Les."

"Les told you where I was?" Well, she couldn't get mad about that. She hadn't told Les her destination should be kept from anyone. "Was there a reason you wanted to see me?"

Sloan nodded. "Two reasons. First, I'm sure you heard inside about the dog pack killing sheep. Everyone's talking about it, so you couldn't have missed it."

"I heard. Does it concern me?"

"No. I wouldn't expect someone who hates sheep as much as you do to be concerned just because there are six hundred sheep on your ranch and a pack of wild dogs roaming the area."

Maggie bristled. "Oh, please. Let's not get all sanctimonious about it, Sloan. If my cattle were in danger, would you be concerned?"

"Yes, but I doubt if you'll believe that."

"Well, I'm not going to stand here and argue with you about it. What's your second reason?"

His gaze pinned her. "Did you hear the thunder last night around midnight?"

Maggie flushed again. "It didn't thunder here."

"Well, it thundered in Wyoming." He paused, then said in a softer tone, "I'll never hear thunder again without thinking of you."

She wouldn't ever hear thunder without thinking of him, either. But just what did he want from her? It would be a long time before she forgot the fury he'd driven her to again and again over his damned sheep. Even if she was beginning to see the absurdity of that old animosity between sheep and cattle people, the personal battles between her and Sloan over the matter weren't that easily dismissed. And it was still two and a half months before that wretched lease expired!

She glared at him. "Maybe I did hear thunder in the night. But if you're fishing to find out if I swooned with sentimentality over it, your line's in the wrong pond. Good night." Maggie swept past him. Or she tried to. Sloan was upright and blocking her path in a flash.

His eyes were hard, she saw with an inward flinch. "You won't let yourself like me, will you?" he said, and Maggie heard anger in his voice.

"*Let* myself? I don't know about you, but I don't sit around and decide who I'm going to like. It's something that just happens all on its own."

"Maggie, that's a crock. You're like two different women. Part of you is intelligent and sensual and full of love, and the other part is making a career out of clinging to foolish old prejudices. Damn, don't you feel just a little pressure from such conflicting personalities?"

That stung, and Maggie's face burned. "Well, aren't you the psychoanalyst," she jeered. "Don't second-rate analyze me, Sloan. I could easily do the same with you."

"No, you couldn't. Not with any accuracy, you couldn't. You won't let yourself know me enough to—"

"Oh, not with any accuracy, you couldn't. You won't let yourself know me enough to—"

"Oh, I know you, all right. Ten years ago—"

"Good Lord! What in hell was so terrible about a kiss?"

Eyes blazing, chin stubbornly set, Maggie let her old grudge spew out. "You had the honor of a...a polecat! You were dating a friend of mine, if you care to remember!"

"So? Dating someone doesn't automatically turn you to stone, does it?"

"Oh, you weren't stone, believe me!"

Sloan's eyes narrowed. "And neither were you. You liked it, Maggie, just as you liked making love during that storm."

"You...you..."

"Stop sputtering. Let me make one thing clear. I don't owe you or anyone else an explanation of that kid's kiss ten years ago, but I'll give you one anyway. Helen and I were never a serious couple, never. And if she was your friend, as you claim, she must have told you that."

Maggie didn't remember it that way. "Helen talked about you all that summer. She liked you," she said accusingly.

His voice was suddenly low and heated. "And I liked you. I liked your snapping black eyes and the way you laughed. I liked your wiry little body, and your long legs in tight jeans. Just like you're wearing tonight. You reached out to me ten years ago, Maggie, and you're still doing it. Yes, I kissed you, and I'm not apologizing for it, either. A man doesn't have to apologize for falling for a woman, but I'll tell you something, sweetheart. You just might do a little thinking about why you melt when I kiss you, when you're so damned positive you want nothing to do with me."

"Apparently you think you've got it figured out. Suppose you tell me!"

"All right, I will. You're falling in love with me."

"*What?*" Maggie didn't know whether to laugh or shriek. Sloan occupied her thoughts far too much of the time, and yes, certainly she'd questioned her abandoned participation during that storm. But love? Not once had she put Sloan and love together. It struck her fast and with the impact of a ton of bricks that he'd been doing that with her, though. My Lord, was *he* falling in love with her?

"No," she mumbled, denying the charge while she stepped backwards. She darted around the back of her car then, circling it to reach the driver's door without going through Sloan. It was a futile evasion, because as she snatched at the door handle, he was right behind her. She could feel his heat on the back of her neck, even without contact. "Go away," she whispered.

"I never thought you were a coward," he said softly, and felt her try to shake off the hand he laid on her shoulder. "Turn around."

"No. Leave me alone."

"Why are you afraid?"

Afraid? It angered Maggie to realize that he'd targeted her feelings so well. She did turn then. "There's no room in my life for a man right now. I don't want an affair, not with you, not with any man. My life is just now going in the direction I've always wanted it to. I've got a dozen plans and years of hard work ahead of me. Don't misunderstand. I love it, every bone-wearying facet of it. I want to raise the best Angus and the best Thoroughbreds in the state, maybe in the country."

Sloan had listened without moving. When she stopped for a breath, he said, "And nothing else is important? Maggie, you're a woman, too, with a woman's passion and needs. What about that?" He ignored her glare and slid his hand under her hair to the back of her neck. At her involuntary shiver, he whispered, "What about this?"

"You think you're going to push me into something, don't you?"

"I'm not going to give up without a fight, if that's what you mean."

His fingers caressed her neck under her hair, and Maggie felt goose bumps pop out on her skin. That taunting flame in her stomach was getting close to unbearable, too, a sensation that for all its discomfort, had a strange drawing power. She had to fight it, she knew, with any weapon she could come up with. She'd defended herself enough; it was time for an offensive attack.

"All right, let's get to the bottom of this. And don't mince words, please. Just what do you want from me?"

Sloan never even skipped a beat. "Your friendship will do for starters."

"Oh, come on. You're standing here with your hand under my hair, doing your best to incite something personal between us, and you expect me to believe all you want is friendship?"

His eyes darkened. "You're right. I want a lot more than friendship. I want you. Like this." He moved closer, pressing his body to hers. The car was at Maggie's back. She felt him steady her head, and then he kissed her. His mouth opened over hers, and her mind exploded into a million dazzling pieces.

His free hand roamed, sliding over the silk of her blouse, down to the taut denim covering her hips. She could feel his hardness and knew he'd already been aroused before the kiss. She didn't want to admit it, but she knew she had been, too. That heat in her lower body wasn't as blatant an advertisement as a man's body, but it had to be as influencing.

He raised his head. "Like that, Maggie. That's what I want from you." His voice was thick, his words ragged. "And you want the same damned thing."

She was breathing hard and trying not to. His face was so close his features blurred, and his body was still molded to hers. But even as she responded to him, he infuriated her. He was so smugly confident, so masculinely sure of himself. And their battles over sheep and a ten-year-old disloyalty were irrevocable.

Too many conflicting emotions resulted in anger. "Take your hands off me," she demanded, and to her surprise, he did. She smoothed down her hair in a rebellious gesture. "It's amazing that you think you can manhandle me anytime you feel like it."

"It's amazing that you think you're fooling anyone."

Her eyes sparked. "You're still a sheepman, Sloan, and that's just about the lowest form of life I know," she hurled, then nearly blacked out as the insult sank into her own brain. God, where had it come from? Even when she'd first seen sheep on the Holloway ranch and been nearly overcome with indignant resentment, she hadn't thought of anything quite that degrading.

It was too late to take it back, she saw. Sloan had physically recoiled. Something sighed in Maggie. She'd succeeded exceptionally well in convincing Sloan he was wrong about her. She nervously watched his recovery, the masculine pride that replaced a fleeting hurt, then saw him nod several times.

"I do believe I'm finally getting the message." His smile didn't quite reach his eyes. "I'm kind of thickheaded sometimes, no doubt because of my long association with sheep. Cattle people are much brighter, and I have the bad habit of forgetting that every so often."

He raised his forefinger to his temple in a mocking salute. "I'll be around your ranch a little more often, ma'am, but only because my poor dumb animals are in danger until that dog pack is hunted down. I understand that the sheriff is getting up a hunting party this week, so the whole problem should be alleviated very soon. In the meantime, I'll do my best to stay out of your sight, ma'am, because while cattle people are so much brighter than sheepers, they're also extremely sensitive. And I sure wouldn't want to bruise your sensitivities."

Frozen in place, Maggie stared after he'd turned and walked away. His long legs swiftly carried him back to Shannon's front door, and he disappeared into the din inside. She wet her dry lips and came out of what felt like a trance, then looked around, sharply aware of her surroundings. The parking lot seemed mundane, a strange drop from the plane of emotion she'd been on. Sounds rolled into her stunned brain again, music from the building, the slam of car doors, voices, laughter.

She'd wounded a man whose most serious crime was wanting her. How could she have said such a thing? Even if she felt that strongly about sheepmen, which she didn't, how could she have thrust the knife so deeply? She'd struck a fatal blow, when all she'd ever wanted...

No, she had to face it. Deep inside, she'd been waiting for the opportunity to pay him back for that humiliation in front of his hired man. She'd attempted it that Sunday evening during the storm, and Sloan had neatly turned the tables on her.

Well, it was over now. She wouldn't have to ever worry again about Sloan bothering her.

Maggie got in her car, but instead of starting it, she put her head down on the steering wheel. The evening hadn't worked out at all. She'd hoped for nothing more than a few hours of relaxation, and instead had heard from a man who

knew Bert Holloway all too well that Bert would return to
his ranch before the end of summer, then had gotten into
that horrible scene with Sloan.

Sighing listlessly, Maggie finally put the key in the ignition.

Seven

For two weeks Maggie saw nothing more of Sloan than an occasional glimpse of his black pickup. She told herself each time that the break between them was best. But no amount of attempted righteousness on the matter made her feel better about what she'd said to him in Shannon's parking lot. An argument was one thing; shredding a man's self-esteem was a whole different ball game. She doubted that even a heartfelt apology would do any good, and whenever Sloan's pickup came tootling up the long driveway and turned off to the main pasture, Maggie recited her little piece—"It's best, it's definitely best."—and went about her business.

There was plenty of business to go about, too. Along with working with Les, Maggie had bought the three mares she'd been negotiating a price on and also attended another cattle auction. Driving home from the auction she acknowledged that she was going to have to make a change at the ranch. With another hundred head of Angus scheduled for delivery, it galled Maggie that she was going to have to face one more defeat at Sloan's hands. The main pasture simply could not support another hundred animals. She would either have to move those damned sheep again or move her cattle.

If she touched Sloan's sheep it would mean another battle. In a way, Maggie was tempted. It was her ranch, after all, and it would do no more harm to his sheep to inhabit another pasture than it would do to her Angus. But the issue was so sensitive now. And in all honesty, Maggie knew why. If she would have talked to Sloan before moving his sheep the first time, he probably would have told her to go ahead. Her anger had caused her to make a mistake in judgment, and in retaliation, Sloan had taken a stand. Now, after the nasty insult she'd given him in Shannon's parking lot, Maggie knew Sloan wouldn't cooperate on this latest problem with their animals.

No, she would just have to move the Angus to another pasture. Sloan's sheep would have the best grass on the ranch all to themselves!

Sloan stopped his pickup where he always did when he came to the Holloway ranch to check on his sheep, right next to a stock gate near the road. He got out, approached the gate and stopped dead in his tracks. Before he could assimilate the absence of cattle in the big field, he heard a far-off bawling.

Following its direction with a curious gaze, he spotted Maggie and Les, each on horseback, herding the cattle in a westerly direction. They were a long ways away and still moving.

Sloan almost couldn't believe his eyes. Maggie had given up completely and left the best pasture on the place to him? How come?

Frowning, Sloan tried to figure Maggie Holloway out. Not for the first time, by any means. Maggie baffled him. He would have bet anything he had that she wouldn't give up on the main pasture battle for love or money. He'd never met a more stubborn woman—no, make that *person*—and yet, there she was, her and Les, driving her Angus to another field.

The question was, why now? Actually it never had made any sense for nearly all of the animals on the place to be cooped up in one area when the ranch had so many unused fields. Of course Maggie was right about this big pasture having the best grass. But several of the other pastures were good, too. No, it wasn't a matter of grass. The fight had been about power.

It still was.

Sloan stared off at the distant tableau of moving cattle and horses. He could tell which rider was Maggie and which was Les, and his gaze narrowed on the smaller figure in a white shirt. "Just what are you up to now, Maggie Holloway?" he whispered.

Maggie slapped her hat against her leg to shake the dust from it as she walked from the barns to the house. She was exhausted, hot and dirty. But she also felt like celebrating. The fence repairs were all done, one chore she was darned glad to have behind her. It had taken weeks, but it was over and done with, and she and Les could finally go on to another project.

Which one? Maggie had a mental list, and she went over it for a minute, then shook her head. She was too tired to think about it now. After a shower...

She stopped. Sloan's pickup was roaring in. He screeched to a halt, jumped out and slammed the door hard. Maggie stared. His face was dark with fury. She could even see rage in his walk! Damn, what now? she thought wearily.

"All right, what the hell did you do with them this time?" he thundered, covering the distance between them in long, loping strides.

Maggie brushed some strands of hair away from her face with the back of her hand and felt the grit of dust and sweat on her forehead. "What did I do with what?"

Sloan smirked right in her face. "Oh, so we're going to play games about it?"

Maggie took an impatient breath. "Just stop it, Sloan. I'm so tired I can't see straight, and I'm in no mood for another round with you."

"Well, that's just too damned bad! I'm not exactly in the best of moods, either. Where'd you put them this time?"

A little bulb went on in Maggie's head. "Are you talking about your sheep, by any chance?"

Sloan rocked back on his bootheels and drawled sarcastically, "No, I'm talking about a herd of elephants." His voice rose. "Hell, yes, I'm talking about my sheep! What'd you do with 'em, Maggie?"

She almost laughed at his theatrics, but she still couldn't completely comprehend. "You mean your sheep are gone?"

He rolled his eyes and groaned a very put upon, "Oh, good Lord."

"Sloan, if your sheep aren't in that pasture and you didn't move them, then someone took them."

"And we both know who, don't we?" he returned with a false, completely snide smile.

Maggie did laugh then, a brief laugh of disbelief. "Listen to me, I did *not* move your sheep. If they're gone, then someone rustled..." She made a face, one that she knew darned well would irk him. "Now that's a stupid idea. Why would anyone bother to rustle sheep?"

"That's cute, Maggie, really cute. But this isn't funny. A good third of my herd is missing. Where did you put 'em? Dammit, am I going to have to get on a horse and go look for them?"

Maggie glanced in the direction of the main pasture, although she couldn't see it from where they were standing. "You're serious? A third of your herd is really gone?"

"Aw, hell," Sloan muttered disgustedly. "Where's Les?"

"At his house. Why?"

"Well, I'm sure not getting anything out of you, am I?"

"Well, you're not going to get anything out of him, either! Why would Les know any more about your damned sheep than I do? Look, I'm not lying and I'm not kidding. I did not, and Les did not, move any of your sheep!"

Sloan backed up a step. His hands went to his hips, and he gave Maggie a relentless stare. "Stare all you want to," she snapped. "I didn't touch your damned sheep! I moved my cattle two days ago, and I haven't even been near that pasture since."

"Well, my sheep are gone!" he yelled.

"So? Is that my fault?"

"It sure as hell is someone's fault!"

"Your lease doesn't require a Holloway to stand guard on your nasty little beasts!"

"You hate my sheep, and you're at the bottom of whatever happened to them!"

"Don't be absurd!"

"I warned you, Maggie. I'm going to the sheriff about this."

"So, go! I wish you would! I wish you'd go somewhere, and in fact, if you really want to do me a favor, you can go straight to hell!"

Les, apparently alerted by the yelling, came out of his house and began walking toward them. "Hey, hey, what's going on?" he called.

Maggie was just about to the end of her rope. She was sweaty, dusty, bone-weary and mad. "This . . . this sheeper thinks I moved his stupid animals!"

"Well, you did it before!" Sloan put in harshly.

"Well, I didn't do it this time!" Maggie shrieked.

"Now, now," Les cautioned as he walked up. "Screaming isn't going to help. Sloan, what happened?"

Sloan looked at the older man. "Some of my sheep are missing, Les."

"That wild dog pack, you think?"

"No. Those dogs were captured over a week ago. I'm talking about two hundred animals."

"Two hundred!" Les gave Maggie a puzzled look, which grated on her nerves.

"Don't look at me, Les. I don't know any more about it than you do," she cried. "Sloan, this is ridiculous. Why would I move only part of your herd?"

"You might take a notion to do most anything," he snarled. "I don't trust you, Maggie. Not where my sheep are concerned."

Maggie struggled with her temper. Cattle rustling was one hazard of ranching that she'd given little thought to, yet she knew very well that it was a much too common occurrence. But sheep? She honestly didn't know if sheepmen were plagued by the same problem. Maybe they were, she thought. Maybe that was one of the reasons Sloan checked his herd so often.

Ignoring Sloan's last insulting remark, she stormed, "There's no point in standing here arguing. I'm going out to that pasture and take a look around." She glared at Sloan. "Did you bother to look for tire tracks?"

"Why? Did you move the herd with a truck?"

"Oh, stop! If you had one ounce of sense you'd be worried about something important. If you really are missing sheep, they were stolen, not moved!" She turned to Les. "Come on, Les. Let's go and see the scene of the crime for ourselves."

Sloan started for his pickup. "Ride with me," he said coldly. He still didn't believe Maggie, even though she should be in the running for a best-actress-of-the-year award.

Maggie almost refused. But it really didn't matter how they got out to the main pasture, so she climbed into Sloan's pickup. The two men got in right behind her.

Sloan's profile was grim and tight-lipped while he drove. Two hundred missing animals was no laughing matter, and he saw nothing funny in Maggie carrying her joke or revenge, or whatever the hell her shenanigans were supposed to be, this far.

Les spoke up. "Two hundred sheep don't just disappear. When did you last check on the herd, Sloan?"

"Two days ago." He gave Maggie a hard glance. "The day you two were moving the cattle. Just why did you move them, by the way?"

Maggie glared right back at him. "Because I bought another hundred Angus, and with *your* animals taking up the main pasture, there wasn't room for them, that's why!"

At the stock gate, Sloan slammed on the brakes and cut the engine. They all scrambled out of the truck. Maggie could see at once that the herd was smaller than it had been, and she went to the fence with a frown. She was aware of Les beside her and then Sloan. "This is terrible," she said under her breath.

"I'd say so," Sloan muttered darkly.

Maggie gave him a dirty look, then started looking around at the ground. There were tire tracks all over the place. Trucks had delivered her Angus, and Sloan was in and out of there every few days with his pickup. It would be impossible to sort one set of tracks from another. "Is sheep rustling very common?"

"I've never been hit," Sloan replied coldly.

"Well, you've been hit now," she drawled with stinging sarcasm. Then, reflectively, her gaze went back to the remaining sheep. "I wonder if the rustlers were after sheep at all. Maybe when they saw the cattle gone, they thought sheep were better than nothing."

Sloan exploded. "Your damned cattle aren't any more valuable than my sheep! Two rams are missing, for your information, and each one of them is worth at least five thousand."

Maggie raised an eyebrow. "Dollars?"

Spinning, Sloan walked away. He was trying to keep calm, but Maggie wasn't making it easy. Poor Les seemed stunned, he saw, and because of him, Sloan began to wonder. "Level with me, Les," he said quietly. "Did I really lose two hundred sheep or did Maggie do something with them?"

"I heard that!" she yelled.

Sloan shot her a dark glower. "I don't give a damn if you did or not. I'm talking to Les."

The older man shook his head. "Sloan, your sheep aren't on the ranch. Not that I know of. If I were you, I'd call the sheriff."

Maggie walked up. "Satisfied?" she asked Sloan coldly.

His eyes bored into her. "You don't care if I call the sheriff?"

"Why should I care? Someone stole your sheep, and if you're ready to talk about it sensibly, I'd like to ask Les if he heard anything unusual during the past two nights. Did you, Les?"

Les shook his head slowly. Maggie frowned. "Neither did I. But I've been so tired at night I've slept like the dead. My Lord, they were bold. Just think about it. Two hundred sheep are a lot of animals to move. They had to bring the trucks right to this gate, because there's no sign of the herd being walked to another loading location."

Sloan studied her, still not quite certain she wasn't pulling something. Maggie sensed the stare and looked into his eyes, and the suspicion and mistrust she saw gave her a start. "I had nothing to do with it," she said quickly, defensively, then realized she'd just defended herself against something abominable, out-and-out thievery! "Sloan, you certainly don't think I *allowed*, or knew about...!" She threw up her hands. "Oh, I don't believe this, I simply do not believe it!"

Sloan turned and looked at the roof of the house. It wasn't that far away, separated from the pasture by only a stand of trees. "Sounds carry at night," he said angrily. "It's hard to believe you wouldn't have heard something."

Maggie was appalled. Never in her entire life had her integrity ever been questioned. She was scrupulously honest. If a clerk made a mistake in her favor with change, she returned it. If she was undercharged, she called attention to it and paid the correct amount. If she found something, which happened occasionally on campus, a scarf or a pair of gloves, she went out of her way to locate the article's owner.

For the first time in her life she felt the guilt of the unjustly accused, the unfairness of having to defend herself against something she wasn't even capable of doing. She looked at Les and saw a similar reaction. The poor man was in misery. "Les," she said weakly. "Please go to the house and call the sheriff. We've got to clear this up."

Sloan's head snapped around, and he narrowed his gaze on Maggie. "I didn't say either of you were involved, Maggie."

"You're thinking it," she said dully. "I've been meaning to get a dog. A dog might have alerted us. We used to have several good watch dogs, but..." Her voice trailed off. "I'll call the sheriff myself." She started away, heading for the trees.

"Wait, I'll drive you back," Sloan called.

"No...no, thank you." She kept on walking.

Les moved closer to Sloan. "Let her go. I know Maggie, and she wants to be alone right now."

Sloan rubbed the back of his neck. He hadn't intended accusing anyone of anything but moving his sheep. When he'd seen the smaller herd and understood that a good third

of his animals were missing, he'd automatically thought that
Maggie was pulling another one of her stunts. One thing had
led to another, and now...?

Sloan muttered a curse. His feelings for Maggie were
sorely tried every time they saw each other, and still they
survived. She had a sharp tongue, and some of her insults
were beyond reason. But he didn't doubt her honesty. Nor
Les's.

He looked the older man in the eye. "I'm sorry, Les. I
know damned well you or Maggie would have raised hell if
you'd heard anything."

Les perked up. "We sure would have, Sloan."

"Let's go back to the house."

"Sure."

It was after dark before the two deputy sheriffs finished
up. They'd written a report on the missing animals, but they
hadn't been very encouraging about getting them back.
"This looks like the work of professionals," had been their
opinion. "Your sheep are probably already in another
state."

Maggie was half-sick over the whole thing. Thieves—
rustlers—stealing stock, virtually from under her nose, was
a terrible blow, a violation of the security she'd always felt
on the ranch. What's more, if she hadn't moved her Angus
when she had, it might be her, instead of Sloan, who was
pale with a victim's frustration.

Actually she was pale anyway. At least Sloan's animals
had been insured. Her Angus weren't. Nor were the Thoroughbreds. It was an oversight she would take care of in the
morning. It hadn't even occurred to her to insure her stock
against rustlers. She was positive—from memory and the
ranch's records—that the Holloways had never carried that
kind of insurance.

Les left right after the deputies, and Maggie stood at the
door with Sloan. She felt awful, and part of it was caused

by the way they kept hurting each other. Today he'd practically accused her of stealing, but that really wasn't any worse than the way she had cut him down in Shannon's parking lot.

It was just best if they stayed away from each other, she thought again, and wished with all her might that the grazing lease didn't have another two months to run.

Oh, why was he looking at her like that?

Maggie tore her gaze from the blue eyes that said there was something she'd be better off not hearing just hanging on the tip of his tongue. "Good night, Sloan," she said, quietly but firmly.

He was holding his hat, turning it. "Maggie, I'm sorry."

"So am I. But we continually rile each other."

"Why? Don't you ask yourself why?"

Her eyes snapped back to his. "It's not because I'm... Or you're..."

"Falling in love?" he said softly.

"How can you even think such a thing? Do people who are falling in love normally dig at each other the way we do? Look at what I said to you that night at Shannon's."

He looked down at his hat. "I'll admit it hurt. But you didn't really mean it, any more than I meant to accuse you of being a sheep rustler."

"A sheep rustler!" Maggie repeated the term incredulously, then started to laugh. "A sheep rustler. Me." It really was absurd to think of herself and sheep rustling in the same breath, and she was glad she could laugh about it now. It hadn't been so funny a few hours ago, she recalled.

But she didn't want to dwell on her feelings at the pasture. In fact she wanted to clear her conscience about that terrible remark she'd made at Shannon's. "Sloan, what I said that night has really been bothering me. I'm sorry."

Her apology was sincere, but then something devilish struck her and she couldn't resist saying it. "A sheepman isn't the lowest form of human life, a sheep *rustler* is."

Sloan threw back his head and laughed, really laughed. When his laughter died, a smile remained, and on impulse he stuck his hand out. "Let's be friends, Maggie."

She eyed the big hand, a little suspiciously, a little hopefully. "I'm not sure we can be," she said truthfully.

"We won't know if we don't try."

Maggie hesitated while every moment they'd spent together flashed through her mind, starting with that kiss ten years before. Then she made up her mind and gave Sloan Prescott the first genuine smile of their relationship. "You're right." She put her hand out and felt his curl around it. An instantaneous echo of intimacy charged through her body, and she hoped it didn't reach her eyes. She didn't want him to know how strongly a simple handshake affected her.

Sloan held her hand longer than he had to. It was firm and warm and he could feel some callouses on her palm. He wanted more than a handshake and she couldn't help knowing that, not when he'd made it so plain in Shannon's parking lot. But all in good time. They weren't ready for anything more tonight. She was tired and so was he, and he was satisfied with the handshake for now. It was a start, and perhaps more meaningful than anything else they'd shared.

"Good night," he said softly.

"Good night, Sloan."

Eight

Maggie paid a visit to her insurance agent the next morning, and she also made inquiries among friends about a dog. Ranchers couldn't stand night guard on their animals, which was why most ranches had several dogs, besides any small house pets. A good ranch dog roamed its territory, and Maggie felt certain that if she'd had a dog, whoever had stolen Sloan's sheep wouldn't have had such an easy time of it.

At the same time she didn't want a vicious animal. The dogs that had recently gone wild and killed sheep had probably been vicious to begin with, she figured. She didn't want to start with a puppy, either, as she wanted immediate protection.

However, she hadn't counted on two dogs. But when she visited a small rancher, who was selling out and moving to town, Maggie knew at first sight of Bonnie and Clyde, a pair of handsome black Labradors, that she couldn't break up the set. Which, she quickly found out, wasn't an option anyway.

To her surprise the rancher interrogated her. He was willing to give the dogs away as a set only, but he was determined they have a good home. "If you don't mind," he said in a way that made Maggie think he didn't really care if she minded or not, "I'll come by your place before we decide."

"That will be fine, Mr. Jamison. Bonnie and Clyde would have a good home with me, but I understand your concern."

In between all the errands she had to attend to, and then during the drive back home, Maggie kept thinking of Sloan. Their relationship had advanced—it seemed like an advance to Maggie—to a whole different level, one that seemed a lot more far-reaching than the turbulent kisses and lovemaking they'd shared.

It made Maggie's lips curve in a faint, partially wry, partially perplexed smile to envision friendship with Sloan. They'd never just talked or eaten together or taken a horseback ride together. The sum total of their interaction consisted of either wild, stormy passion or arguments. Had she changed so much in two months that neither sheep nor the past were all that important now? she wondered.

Two months? It gave Maggie a start to realize that two months of the summer were gone. The weeks had flown by, with every day but Sundays having been spent in hard work. The place showed it, too. Her parents wouldn't recognize the ranch when they came for a visit.

A visit that was coming up very soon. Every time Maggie remembered that Bert would be campaigning in southern Montana shortly, her stomach knotted. Not that she didn't want to see her parents. She would welcome some time in their company. She would enjoy hearing from both of them of their state-wide travels. But she couldn't kid or talk herself out of the gnawing worry that Bert would suddenly lose interest in politics and, like Jake Barnett had put it, "skedaddle for home."

It didn't help Maggie's uneasiness to remember that she had talked her parents into the sale. In actuality, she had sold them on the idea. After every telephone conversation she felt better, because neither Bert nor Sarah ever sounded the least bit disenchanted with politics or travel. But after a few days, doubts would besiege Maggie again.

It seemed like there was always something to worry about, Maggie thought as she turned into the ranch's driveway. When had she become such a worrywart? Just when she had the ranch in near apple-pie order, there was the situation—maybe only imagined, she hoped—with Bert and Sarah.

And there was Sloan. There was a kind of nebulous connection with Sloan to deal with, something deep inside Maggie that warmed when he came to mind. It seemed important, forming a foundation for questions that Maggie had never had to face before. Was she developing serious feelings for a man? Was she beginning to think of her marital future? Owning and operating the ranch was wonderful, but what about her personal life? What about marriage, children?

It astounded Maggie that she was thinking about those things because of Sloan. Their relationship had been so rocky, even that brief episode ten years before.

But could it be more? Could this stab at friendship, combined with the undeniable sexuality between them, result in something serious? Getting right to the heart of the matter, was she putting aside that old issue of what Sloan did for a living versus the Holloways' pride in what they did? Trying to be fair, Maggie attempted to squeeze the old prejudice down to just her and Sloan. It wasn't easy to forego the many memories she had of her grandfather's vociferous intolerance of sheep and sheepherders, but when she halfway succeeded and searched her own conscience, it was plain that she wasn't happy with bigotry of any kind.

Maggie's thoughts continued in that vein while she parked and unloaded the car. She'd stopped at the grocery store and had several bags of fresh produce, dairy products and bakery goods to carry in. Then, still pensive, she went out to see how Les was coming with the project she'd started him on that morning.

The large barn was a major undertaking. Maggie had left it and the house until last. The house *would* be last, she'd decided, because the house would never make the ranch operation one thin dime. Scraping and painting it would merely be a cosmetic improvement, which was needed to complete the renovations, to be sure. But the barn was an important structure, and she'd started Les on repairing some leaky spots in the roof that morning.

It was late afternoon now, and walking down to the barn, Maggie could see Les on the roof, still hammering new shingles in place. She stood on the ground and called up, "Still hard at it? How's it coming?"

"Hi, Maggie. There's just one more spot to patch, then I'll be finished. We should be able to start scraping the old paint off this building in the morning."

"Good. I think I found us a dog, Les. Two dogs, actually. They're two-year-old black Labs. I'll know for sure in a couple of days."

"Hey, that's great! Oh, by the way, Sloan was here earlier."

Maggie's heart skipped a beat. "Just to check on the sheep?"

"Well, he did that, too. But he asked for you. I told him you'd be back some time this afternoon, and he said he'd see you tonight."

"Oh. Tonight. Fine." Was it fine? Was it *really* fine? Frowning, Maggie invited Les to have dinner with her, then started back to the house. She was going to have the opportunity to test all of the theories and suppositions she'd wrestled with all day, she realized. Sloan would come at night for only one reason, to expand on that friendship he'd urged her to try.

Maggie was sitting on the patio, watching the sun going down. Les had eaten with her, then gone to his own little house. On the still, quiet air, Maggie could hear faint evidence of Les's TV set, a drift of music and voices coming through his open windows. It was a pleasant summer's evening, a peaceful time of day. But the peace didn't quite reach Maggie's inner disquietude. Outwardly she was calm, appearing serene in an unadorned white sundress and sandals; inwardly she felt expectant, anxious.

She tried not to look on Sloan's impending visit as a date. In the true sense of the word, a casual drop-in call wasn't a date. Yet, Maggie felt a strange breathlessness, a sense of waiting.

When she heard a vehicle approaching, her pulse quickened and then, almost immediately, leveled out. She'd come to know the sound of Sloan's pickup, and the low purr she could hear was uniquely different.

Rising slowly, Maggie started across the lawn, wondering who was stopping by. Friends from Newley and neighboring ranches stopped in for a hello now and again, and, too, it could be someone for Les.

Maggie blinked as a shiny clean, navy-blue Jaguar sedan pulled up beside the house. To her surprise, Sloan climbed out. "Did you get a new car?" she asked as she walked over to him.

"I've had the Jag about two years now," he replied with a broad smile and an admiring light in his eyes. Maggie looked beautiful. Her weeks of working outdoors had tanned her naturally deep-toned skin, and it was stunning against the stark white of her dress. Her black eyes were like bits of satin, and she was wearing a dusty rose blusher on her cheeks and a hint of matching lipstick.

"Oh, I assumed... I mean, since I hadn't seen it before..."

"I only use it for pleasure."

For pleasure. The words brought a tide of warmth to Maggie's neck and face, and she quickly bent over and peered into the Jag's interior. It had plush, navy seats and a beautifully intricate dashboard. "I've always admired Jaguars."

"Want to take a ride?"

She laughed. "I wasn't hinting." The Jag wasn't the only surprise. Sloan was wearing pale gray slacks, a darker gray shirt and black loafers. His thick, dark hair was neatly brushed and he smelled positively wonderful. He was outrageously handsome, and also looked as far from a rancher—sheep *or* cattle—as any man she'd ever seen. Maggie wondered if he was intentionally showing her another side of himself, one she hadn't even suspected existed. It made her a little giddy to think that Sloan just might be courting her, giddier still to recognize her response to that likelihood.

"Just once around the block?" Sloan teased. There certainly weren't any blocks to drive around, not unless they headed for Newley and cruised its dozen or so streets. It came to Maggie that she no longer cared if anyone she knew saw her with Sloan. Sheeper or not, he was a respected part of the ranching community.

"All right," she agreed with a smile.

Sloan opened her door and Maggie settled into the luxury car, looking everything over with avid interest. They discussed the Jag for several miles, and Maggie received a lot of technical data that made little sense to her. She wasn't mechanically minded, and the Jaguar was merely beautiful. To her, what went on under its hood was secondary to the car's elegant lines.

They rode with the windows partially open, and the cool evening air ruffled Maggie's hair. Sloan brought the conversation to a personal level after a companionable silence, startling Maggie with, "I made some inquiries about Helen White, Maggie."

Her eyes grew large and curious. She couldn't have imagined Sloan bringing up Helen this way. "Helen lives in Denver."

"You know?"

"Her aunt goes to the same church I attend. I got Helen's address from her so I could drop her a line."

"And did you?"

"No," Maggie admitted with a touch of guilt. "I've been so busy that I've neglected a lot of correspondence, I'm afraid."

Sloan sent his passenger a glance. "But you do know that Helen's been married for years and has three children?"

"Yes. Sloan..."

He heard reluctance in her voice. "No, please don't sweep it under the carpet. It's important, Maggie. That old incident set the tone of our present relationship. When you came to my house that first night, it was on your mind."

"Well, yes," she admitted uneasily.

"It was on my mind, too."

His was a sensual admission, simply because of the way he'd said it. Sloan's memory of that night, as he'd pointed out before, was different than hers, Maggie saw. For the first time she wondered exactly how he did see it. "All right. If you want to talk about it, I'm willing."

He gave her a quick, warm smile. "Good." His gaze returned to the road. "I met Helen through mutual friends. Then I met you through Helen."

"True," she murmured.

He laughed then, a brief sound with little mirth. Maggie responded with a sharp glance. "You hit me hard, Maggie. Did you have any idea how you affected me? I tried to make friends, but you were the most standoffish little thing I'd ever met."

"You were my friend's boyfriend!"

"Now there's where we disagree. Helen and I dated no more than three or four times."

"Sloan, Helen liked you a lot."

"And I liked Helen. But that's all it was, liking. You aroused other kinds of feelings, *adult* feelings, Maggie. You know," he mused aloud, "in retrospect, I think you were my first serious crush."

Her heart went out to him, for the impulsive young man he'd been, for the way she'd lit into him for stealing a kiss. But her fury hadn't been only because of Helen, she recalled. There'd been the matter of how her grandfather would have perceived a liaison with a sheepman. Even more influencing, though, had been how soul-deep staggered she'd been by feelings she'd never come close to before. Sloan had nearly knocked her socks off with that kiss. She understood it now, but at a rather naive eighteen, churning, pressuring desire had frightened her.

"We...were very young," she said quietly, thoughtfully, seeing quite clearly now that Sloan was indeed courting her. Apparently he saw a need to start at their beginning, with that wild kiss and her subsequent anger. She hadn't been kind, and the memory was unsettling.

Sloan had been driving north, avoiding Newley by taking a back road. Maggie knew the area like the palm of her hand, and when he turned off onto another road, she knew where he was heading. Potts Lake was a small body of water with a Scout camp on its eastern shore and about twenty private cabins on its western. In between were several public swimming beaches. They would be all but deserted on a week night, Maggie knew, although on weekends and holidays the public areas were usually crammed with picnickers and campers.

Sloan parked well away from the few other cars and turned off the ignition. It was quite dark, and with the headlights off, Maggie was able to pick out a few lights scattered around the lake, dock lights, cabin lights. "I haven't been out here in years," she said softly.

"It's a good swimming lake."

"Oh, yes." She smiled at memories of teenaged swimming parties. Motorboats and any other gasoline- or diesel-powered craft were banned at Potts Lake, so there was nothing but rowboats, canoes or rubber rafts for swimmers to contend with.

"Maggie..." Sloan turned in the seat, facing her, and stretched his arm along the seat back, not quite touching her.

"Yes?" She heard him draw in a deep breath.

"I think you know how I feel about you," he said in a low, rather hushed voice.

She dampened her lips. "Let's not rush things, please."

He was silent a moment. "Have you ever wondered about my marriage?"

Her gaze went to him and then back to the velvety scene of dark lake water with a reflected moon and distant, twinkling shore lights. "Yes," she admitted. "I've wondered."

"May I tell you about it?"

"Only if you want to, Sloan."

"I'd like to. It started out good, Maggie. The first year was good. And then, everything started changing. Gail was from Connecticut, and she started asking me to sell the ranch and move her back to Hartford. At first I didn't take it seriously. She'd known from our first date how much my family's ranch meant to me. Five generations of Prescotts have lived on that place, and the real trouble began when I started hoping for a sixth."

"Children," Maggie murmured, surprised at the degree of discomfort she was attaining from hearing Sloan speak of his ex-wife. She refused to label it jealousy, because she wasn't by nature a jealous person. But something was spik-

ing her insides while her mind formed images from Sloan's
words, and it wasn't a pleasant feeling.

"I won't go into details, but any affection we started with
was destroyed in two years of fighting. The divorce was bitter, mostly because of Gail's financial demands. It was finally settled, but it left a bad taste. You're the first woman
I've wanted to even spend time with since."

"Oh?" Maggie's heart had begun a faster beat. Sloan's
fingers had wound into her hair, and she could feel each tiny
movement they made reverberating clear to her toes. She
sensed his smile and turned her head to look at him.

"We've fought like cats and dogs, haven't we?" he said
softly.

"Yes."

"But no more, Maggie. Fighting isn't what either of us
wants from the other now."

Her smile was weak. She remembered how effectively
Sloan had demonstrated in Shannon's parking lot what he
wanted from her. Her own feelings weren't that clear.
Something was happening to them, she couldn't possibly
pretend not to realize that. But the strongest caution of her
life was gripping her, maybe because she did suspect that
this could be serious. If it was, there was so much involved.
The ranches, for one major hurdle. Neither of them would
ever want to give up their family's generations-old ground
and live on the other's.

Sloan sensed her ambivalence. "Don't fret about it now,"
he said softly, and slid across the seat. His arms dropped
around her, and Maggie tipped her head back to see his face.
Her eyes were troubled, and Sloan pressed a gentle kiss to
her temple. "I'm not going to pressure you, Maggie. Just let
me hold you," he whispered.

She sighed and dropped her head to his chest. His voice
rumbled quietly beneath her ear. "Is there anyone important in Bozeman?" she heard.

She knew exactly what he meant and answered truthfully. "No, no one important."

They sat without moving for several minutes, Sloan's arms around her, his chin resting on the top of her head. There was passion in the embrace—Maggie could feel it in every cell—but it was controlled, by Sloan, by her. Perhaps more meaningful was a sense of communion and the loveliest warmth of her life pervading her system. It was more than desire, and she knew, without even a thread of doubt, that she had never experienced it before this summer.

She closed her eyes and thought about love and its ramifications. She and Sloan could not have a peaceful future, not when they were so divided in such incontrovertible ways. She was able now to divorce herself—and Sloan—from the old sheep-cattle bias, but their more tangible differences?

He lived in Wyoming, she in Montana. He had his ranch, she had hers. Which of them would even consider making the sacrifice necessary for any sort of permanent arrangement between them?

Maggie felt him seeking her lips, and she relaxed into a kiss she couldn't deny herself. His mouth was undemanding, moving slowly on hers, and her body immediately buzzed with heated awareness. But despite the desire he so easily brought to life, Maggie was beginning to see something that sparked a deeply rooted unhappiness within her. Sloan's first marriage might even have been damaged by his attachment to his ranch, although any woman who married a born and bred country man had to know that he wasn't going to change on a whim.

As for her, Maggie Holloway, only this summer she'd had a dream come to life. Giving up *her* ranch was... unthinkable.

It wasn't a subject she felt she could introduce. Nothing of a future together had even been hinted at, even if she knew that possibly important feelings were developing between them.

Sloan's lips left hers, and he adjusted their position with a sigh that sounded quite contented to Maggie. Her head rested in the crook of his shoulder and arm, a relaxed embrace, giving Maggie reason to believe he really didn't intend any pressure tonight. But she wondered what was in his mind for them. Did he see the pitfalls ahead, as she did?

He spoke quietly. "Talk to me, Maggie. Tell me about your grandfather."

Lyle Holloway was a pleasant topic as far as Maggie was concerned, and she was pleased that Sloan wanted to hear about the man she had doted on while growing up. She related many of her memories, and then asked Sloan about his family. He spoke freely.

His mother had died very young, leaving Sloan an only child to be raised by his father. They'd been close, united in their love of a way of life. Then, two years before Sloan met Gail and married, his father had died. "You're very lucky to have both of your parents living," Sloan told Maggie.

"Yes, I know."

"How is Bert doing in the campaign? I see his name in the newspaper every so often."

For a moment Maggie had to forcibly stifle the impulse to talk about her fear with the ranch and her father. But envisioning putting such an undefined worry into words made it seem silly, and she only said, "Both Mother and Dad seem delighted with the campaign."

"I really like your dad, Maggie. I only spent a few minutes with your mother, but she seems very nice, too."

"Thank you."

Maggie was surprised when Sloan switched on a dome light to check his watch and said that it was after ten. They'd spent several hours together, and not one unpleasant word had been spoken.

Sloan tipped her chin up and softly kissed her lips. "This has been nice, Maggie."

"Yes, it has," she agreed quietly.

His mouth grazed hers again, lightly. Then, with a tender smile, he moved back behind the wheel and started the car.

Maggie's heart was thumping with all sorts of emotions and questions. She realized that she'd been able to deal with the other phases of their relationship much easier than she could with the sweet sensuality that was between them now and growing by such leaps and bounds. She thought of that stormy evening and of their uninhibited lovemaking, and she suddenly knew that Sloan had been ready at that point to begin something serious.

She must have hurt him with her turndown, and still he'd continued to come around. He'd attempted several times to get past it, which, now that she was seeing things in a different light, had to mean that he must care a great deal for her.

They were both heading for heartache, Maggie thought sadly.

"Did you have a good day in town?"

"Pardon?" Maggie's thoughts returned to the present. "Oh, yes." She told him about her errands, ending with the story about the Labrador dogs. "I'm pretty sure that once Mr. Jamison sees the ranch, he'll let me have Bonnie and Clyde."

Sloan chuckled over the dogs's names, and Maggie smiled. Then she grew more serious. "Sloan, do you think the thieves will strike again?"

He shook his head. "Those deputies don't think so. Professional rustlers hit and run. Anyway, Maggie, no one can guard their animals twenty-four hours a day. Rustling is one of the risks of ranching."

"Well, once I get Bonnie and Clyde, no one will be able to sneak around at night without me or Les knowing it. Their barking is loud enough to wake the dead. When I drove up to the Jamison place, I got a very good sample of the noise they can make."

"I saw your Thoroughbred mares today," Sloan said.

Maggie swelled with pride. "Aren't they beautiful? With Rebel as their sire and those mares for dams, the foals have got to be special."

Sloan agreed with a nod of his head. "I think you like the horses best. Am I wrong?"

"No, you're very right. But the Angus will bring in money while I'm expanding the horse-breeding operation." Maggie turned in the seat, one leg crooked beneath her. "Oh, Sloan, I have such great plans. It will take time, but every year will be so rewarding."

"Ranching is rewarding," he agreed with a sidelong glance at her. "You've spent a great deal of money on your stock."

Maggie sensed his curiosity about how she'd managed such extensive purchases, and after thinking about it she decided there was no good reason why she shouldn't explain. "My grandfather left me a nice sum of money, and I had never touched it. My spending is done for this summer, though." Her thoughts went further on the subject. Her bank account was as low as she dare take it, considering the payments she must make to her parents and the cost of general ranch operation. The bottom line was that she had committed everything she had to making her dream a reality.

She wasn't worried about money, though. She had laid out a financial plan, which took into account fall sales of steers and an increased herd during each calving season. It was a sensible workable plan, and barring some unpredictable catastrophe such as the near miss she'd had with the rustlers, should see her through the first and most crucial few years of the business. After that she would be well-established, she figured.

While Sloan drove, Maggie studied him in the dash lights. No, it wasn't money that worried her, she thought. It was Sloan and where the two of them were heading. And also that nagging concern about her parents.

With an abrupt movement, Maggie faced front. She could only assume a wait-and-see attitude with Bert and Sarah, but with Sloan and her, it was becoming a matter of priorities. Her total commitment to the ranch could not be taken lightly. It not only involved emotion now, she'd invested most of her money. She'd also cancelled her teaching contract, making a serious break with her former career.

The absolute truth was, Sloan was the wrong man for a woman with such a strong commitment. He should look for a rancher's daughter, someone who would love his place and not pine for city lights or even her own family's ranch. Maggie's heart was all tied up with Holloway ground.

The thought birthed an astonishingly piercing burst of emotions, and Maggie's eyes sought Sloan again. She—and him, too—were dangerously close to more unhappiness than either of them deserved. Couldn't he see what was happening, and that getting more deeply involved would only magnify the hurt, once they reached that inevitable impasse?

Traveling the ranch's long driveway, Maggie got a renewed sense of pride and satisfaction. She wasn't sure how to present it to Sloan, but she knew she had to tell him that the friendship they had agreed upon last night was all she could give him.

Parking the Jaguar beside the house, Sloan turned off the motor. "Will you have dinner with me tomorrow night?" he asked in the sudden quiet. When she didn't answer, he added, "We could drive to Billings or Sheridan, whichever you'd prefer."

Maggie felt her courage slipping, and only murmured a less than steady, "Not tomorrow night. I'll be scraping paint all day...both Les and me...and I'll probably be exhausted."

Sloan reached out and touched her hair. "You've worked hard here, Maggie. I don't think I've ever known anyone, man or woman, who ever worked any harder. You did what you set out to do. You must feel a great deal of pride in your accomplishments.''

"I do," she admitted without coyness. She had every right to feel pride, and so did Les.

"If not tomorrow night, tell me when. Any evening is fine with me," Sloan said softly.

His fingers in her hair were giving Maggie that warm, weak feeling in the pit of her stomach. But she'd already made her choice, two months before, and she was in too deep with the ranch, both emotionally and financially, to drop everything because of the thrill of a man's touch.

"Sloan," she said quietly. "I have to say something. I feel good because we're not fighting now. I hope we stay friends. But that's all we can be." She felt Sloan's understanding in the sudden unmoving stiffness of the fingers in her hair, and then his hand left her altogether. He was silent and looking out the windshield for a long, tension-filled stretch. Until Maggie sighed and reached for the door handle.

"I swore I wasn't going to pressure you in any way," he said then, and Maggie heard a hard edge on the words. "Apparently you're still coming up with reasons why you and I shouldn't be *more* than friends. I thought we'd made some great headway tonight, but it was obviously a premature conclusion." He looked at her, and Maggie caught the glint of reflected light in his eyes. "Maybe I've beat around the bush just a little too much. Sleep on this, Maggie. I'm in love with you. Now, that might not mean one damned thing to you, but—"

"Sloan! Please don't say any more!" Her stomach was churning. This was what she had feared. When it hadn't been said, she'd been able to at least partially block out the possibility. Now she must face her own feelings, and she wasn't ready to. She didn't *want* to!

She fumbled with the door handle. "Good night."

"I'll walk you to the door."

"No, please! Good night." Quickly Maggie got out of the Jag and closed the door. She was in the house, standing in the dark, before she heard the car start and leave.

Nine

Maggie put in a bad night, one filled with battles over choices and priorities. When she finally left her bed at dawn, it was with nothing resolved. She needed to think in the clear light of day, she felt, and knew she couldn't possibly scrape paint that day.

After putting coffee on to brew, she went outside and walked down to Les's house. She could hear his radio as she knocked on the door, which Les opened with a welcoming grin. "Mornin', Maggie. Come on in and have some coffee."

"Mine's brewing, Les, thanks. I just wanted to tell you to take the day off."

The older man looked surprised. "How come?"

Maggie looked away, then brought a vague, slightly guilty smile back to her hired man. "I'm going to take Rebel out for a long ride. I'll probably be gone most of the day."

"Just feel like playing hookey, huh?" Les teased. "Well, look, Maggie, you go right ahead. I'll get started on scraping that paint. Heck, I don't want a day off. What would I do all day?''

What a change Les had undergone, Maggie marvelled privately. Two months ago anyone would have been hard-pressed to catch the man doing any kind of real work on the ranch. It pleased Maggie immeasurably that Les's pride of workmanship now matched her own.

Or, her own as it usually was. Today her heart wasn't in scraping paint or any other task on the ranch. Today she just wanted to get away by herself. She wanted to ride and think and shore up the perspective that Sloan was gradually un-dermining.

"Thanks, Les. I would like you to start thinking about a couple of weeks off in September, however."

Les rubbed his jaw. "Well, that would be nice. I could visit my sister in Minneapolis."

"With pay, of course," Maggie added, putting gratitude for all of Les's help in a sincere smile.

Les's eyes lit up. "That's mighty nice of you, Maggie. I'll plan on it. As for today, you just go and have a good time. And don't worry about what's going on here. I'll have a good portion of that barn done by tonight."

Maggie walked back to her house with very little trace of the smile she'd bestowed on Les. She felt like she was car-rying a heavy weight in her midsection, and she knew she was going to have to get rid of it if she was to function pro-ductively again.

But just how did a woman purge a man from her system? *Not easily*, Maggie wryly answered herself. It wasn't a matter of merely deciding that she and Sloan had no real chance; she could make decisions until she was blue in the face, but until she actually implemented them, they were meaningless.

Still, how was she to convince Sloan that they were no good for each other when she was having trouble convinc-ing herself? And she could *see* the problems ahead with an almost painful distinction. If he had any such foresight, he wasn't saying so.

Maggie's confusion was the worst of her life, and she concentrated on mundane tasks—breakfast, packing a lunch to take with her, filling a canteen with water, pulling on her riding boots—instead of attempting to unravel it. Later, she thought. Later, when she was away from the house and buildings, when she was completely isolated in the serenity that riding alone usually gave her, she would reason things out.

Around noon Maggie found herself at the little pond she'd often swam in as a youngster and had skinny-dipped in several times this summer. She'd had a marvelous morning's ride and felt physically relaxed, even if she hadn't been struck by a brilliant solution to her emotional quandary.

Rebel was grazing on a long tether so he could also reach the pond for water, and Maggie was sitting in the shade of a massive cottonwood. She had taken off her straw hat, placing it on the grass beside her, and proceeded to unwrap her lunch of cheese, crackers, apples and grapes. She was hungry, she realized, and plucked several grapes and popped them into her mouth, then placed everything within easy reach and settled back against the trunk of the tree to enjoy a leisurely meal.

She felt somewhat better. Riding over her own land, stopping at pretty spots, just basking in the satisfying sensation of ownership, had been a nourishing experience. It was something she should do more often, she decided, admitting at the same time that as hard as she and Les had been working, there'd been no time for such excursions.

From now on she would make the time. It was important, crucial even, that she renew this oneness with her goal. Her plans for the ranch seemed clearer again, didn't they?

Maggie sighed between bites of cheese and gazed off into the distance, not certain that she'd clarified all that much.

Then she frowned and sat up straighter. A horse and rider were barely recognizable, so far off they appeared toylike.

Squinting at the distant sight, Maggie wondered if Les was looking for her. If he was, the reason would be serious. Les wouldn't come after her unless he absolutely had to.

Slowly Maggie got to her feet. She watched the horse and rider for another few minutes, then bent down and gathered up the remains of her lunch. It had to be Les. Who else...?

Sloan?

Standing again, Maggie squinted at the horse and rider again. They were coming in her direction, and yes, the rider could very well be Sloan. An immediate tingling in her body angered Maggie. How could she have so little control over herself to be that susceptible to the mere possibility of Sloan riding up?

What had she gained this morning? Nothing, not a damned thing, she realized disgustedly. By herself, enjoying the ride on Rebel, she'd renewed her zeal for the ranch. But at first sight of Sloan—hell, the rider could *still* be Les— she got all weak-kneed and female again. Damn!

Maggie leaned against the tree and bit into an apple, watching the approaching horse and rider with a resentful expression. It was Sloan, all right. And riding one of her horses, to boot. His progress was determined; he was coming directly to the pond.

The apple was down to its core before Sloan was within calling distance. But neither he nor Maggie said a word. He rode up and dismounted, then said a calm, collected, "Hello."

There was an expression in his blue eyes, something that he'd screened out of his voice, apparently, that reached deep inside Maggie and wrung her out. She couldn't go on living with such ambivalence, she realized, recalling in a flash of events involving the two of them, that she'd been doing just that all summer.

Her voice was sharp, a reflexive defense against her own uncertainty. "I take it you're looking for me?"

Sloan stood with his horse's reins in his hand, and he wasn't in any hurry to answer. Maggie flushed at the perception she saw in his eyes. He *knew* how strongly he affected her!

He walked away then, leading his horse to the pond for a drink. When he returned, Maggie was reasonably controlled. Even if she hadn't sought it, this was an opportunity to make a clean and final break with Sloan, and she didn't want to do it with anger. She watched him toss his hat to the ground, then follow it down, and she sank to the grass, too.

"Les told me you were out riding," he said quietly. "I've been looking for you for about an hour."

"I wanted to be alone."

"We need to talk."

Maggie pulled up a handful of grass and let it dribble through her fingers, studying the falling blades thoughtfully. "Yes, I think we do," she finally replied.

"I'm not going to mince words anymore, Maggie. I love you."

It wasn't a shock today; that had come last night when he'd said it. Yet the words dug deeper into Maggie's brain, forcing her to face them. She raised her eyes to his. "What do you expect me to say to that?"

"Expect, or hope?" His expression pleaded. "Can you be completely honest with me? That's what I need now, Maggie, your honesty."

Maggie hesitated. Could she be honest? Would it even help? What real good would come out of confessing that yes, she had feelings for him when she knew how far apart their futures were? Their lives were similar, stunningly alike, actually. Which, oddly enough, was their biggest obstacle to anything lasting. In a way, she had an almost masculine affinity with her land, certainly paralleling whatever passion and affection Sloan felt for his.

"I'll be honest," she said low. "But let's do a little supposing. I know you're talking about something serious between us. You're an intelligent man. Just how would you propose we deal with our respective ranches?"

"Maggie, if two people really love each other, they can work out *any* problem."

His confident answer didn't surprise Maggie all that much. Her thoughts went in two directions, one questioning just how much or how little love there had been between Sloan and his ex-wife when their "problem" had ended in divorce. The other fork of her thoughts was about the two of them, and how all that confidence Sloan exuded had to be a general attitude. He hadn't worried or probably even given much thought to the ranch situation.

Her eyes took on a challenge. "Do you even see the problem?"

Sloan nodded. "Of course I do. But I see something more important than that, too. Us. You and me." His gaze washed over her. "Maggie, I love you. Tell me if I have a chance. That's why I'm out here. Last night after I left you, I drove around for hours. When I finally went home, I hardly slept. Do you want to know something? I know now that I fell in love with you ten years ago. I'd lost track of it, yes. But who wouldn't have? Ten years is a long time."

"When you were dealing with Dad on the grazing lease, you must have known he was my father," she said skeptically.

"Yes. But it had been so long, and I didn't know you'd be here for the summer."

"I always came home for the summer." Maggie was frowning and plucking stalks of grass, one at a time now.

"But I didn't know that, and I didn't question your father about you. I didn't know if you were married, or what. Remember when I asked you about it?"

Maggie looked off. She remembered that moment very well. It was just before he kissed her in his study, the night she'd gone to his house to discuss the lease. Other memories lined up, every blasted one of them about kisses, and more. Much, much more. This man's body on hers, in hers, was one memory she'd take to her grave.

And into marriage with another man?

The question struck Maggie so hard she closed her eyes. How could she deal with this? Lord above, she cared too much! Common sense was a pitiful substitute for caring. For loving. For being loved.

Her lashes rose slowly. "Oh, Sloan," she whispered brokenly, pure misery in her eyes. "You want honesty? All right, but mine is that I *honestly* don't know what to do about us."

"I do." He reached out to her, and the emotion in his eyes pushed Maggie right up to the edge of her defenses. Her pupils enlarged and her breath stopped in her throat, while, with a hand on her shoulder, Sloan bent forward. His mouth brushed hers. "I know what to do," he said softly. "It's not that complicated, Maggie. Just close your eyes and let me love you."

She felt a hypnotic wave stealing her strength. "That isn't the answer," she whispered.

His mouth feathered against hers again. "To what question?" His voice was a low, persuasive purr, and his hand moved beneath her hair to the back to her neck.

"To..." Her senses were reeling, blurring issues, and she lost her train of thought. Her eyelids drooped and her lips parted, moist and pink and expectant. When his mouth firmly covered hers, she sighed into the kiss, and her hands moved to his chest. Beneath a white cotton shirt his heart beat steady and hard. Maggie felt its rhythm meshing with the throbbing of her own pulse.

The kiss was warm and dizzying, sensual but tinged with sweetness, a loving kiss. Maggie understood then. Even dazed, she understood and believed Sloan's feelings. He really loved her...he was really *in* love with her.

There was a sense of awe in the acknowledgment, and its physical counterpart was a melting sensation. There'd been men who'd carried certain importances before, men she'd respected, liked because of common interests and even loved a little. By the same token Maggie had perceived from them aspects of respect and affection. But never, never had she felt, in every nook and cranny of her being, the power of being truly loved.

It was simultaneously a weakening and energizing feeling. It was also bonding, and Maggie felt herself drawing emotionally closer to Sloan. Physically, his half of the kiss was becoming more insistent, but she didn't push him away or put up any kind of protest.

She couldn't. She was completely lost in the magic of his lips on hers, in the way his big hand moved on the back of her neck. Her skin tingled beneath his palm, sending out a sensually rippling message to every part of her body.

His mouth lifted from hers, and he whispered huskily, "Ah, Maggie. You love me, too, don't you?" He looked into her dazed black eyes. "You're still not ready to say it, are you? But I know anyway. I know, Maggie. It's not something you can conceal."

"Don't. Please," she whispered raggedly. "I'm not ready to..."

When she stopped he questioned softly, "To make that kind of commitment?"

Maggie wasn't exactly bursting with confidence, especially on the subject of commitment. But she managed a weak nod of her head.

Sloan's hand slid around her neck, and his thumb caressed her bottom lip. "You're so pretty." His gaze moved over her face, feature by feature. Maggie found herself doing the same with him. Did any other man have such blue, blue eyes? Their depth seemed to go on forever. His skin was tan and crinkled in lovely spots, at the corners of his eyes, on each side of his mouth. That close to him, Maggie could see isolated strands of silver intermingled with the coarse, rich brown of his hair. He was a handsome man, a pleasing mixture of youthfulness and maturity.

She lingered at the contours of his mouth, and her heart picked up speed. Her hands were still on his chest. She curled her fingers into his shirt, and saw a new light in his eyes. Like the night of the storm, the sexuality between them was expanding, enveloping both of them.

She wanted it to. She wanted him. "Sloan," she whispered breathily, and heard the invitation in her own voice. It was all right, she'd meant it. She might not be ready to talk about commitment, but her body was demanding attention, aching with desire. That searing flame had been rekindled in the pit of her stomach, and she'd lost the will to combat it.

Sloan's response was swift. He brought them both down to the ground, with Maggie on her back and him leaning over her. His mouth was hungry, but he soon discovered that hers was, too. This kiss wasn't sweet. It was inflaming, lustful, erotic.

His right thigh rose to rest on her legs. Her arms were around his neck, her hands feverish on his back and shoulders. His hips rocked the hard masculinity in his jeans against her, and he burrowed a hand under her shirt to caress her breasts.

His tongue was hot in her mouth, but no hotter than her entire body was becoming. Waves of heat raised her temperature, increased again by his palm chafing one nipple, then the other. Their breathing was loud and raspy.

Sloan raised his head. His mouth was wet, his eyes glazed. "Here, Maggie? Right here?"

She touched his face. "Right here," she whispered. They were as alone as any two people could be, under a canopy of green, breeze-ruffled leaves and a sky as blue as Sloan's eyes.

The air smelled of sweet grass and sun-warmed earth, and there was something especially exciting about the thought of making love in the outdoors.

She saw the tremble in his hand as he began to unbutton her shirt, and an anxious little smile curved her lips as she reached for his buttons. He finished first, and ignoring her attempts to bare his chest, bent his head to her breasts.

Maggie moaned softly when his mouth opened around a nipple. His tongue played with it, teased it, and she gave in to the shooting pleasure he was creating. He began to gently suck, and her fingers wove into his hair as pleasure and desire intensified. "Oh, Sloan," she hoarsely whispered.

He went slow, kissing her lips, then her breasts, again and again, and the pressure mounted between them. Somehow she got the rest of his shirt buttons undone, and then, suddenly, their passion seemed to explode. He sat up and pulled his boots and socks off, and dazed, watchful of his movements, Maggie did the same with hers. They stood to shed their tight jeans, and the splendor of their nudity stopped them both for a moment.

Their bodies were suntanned with patches of whiter skin—Sloan's legs were lighter than his chest and arms—Maggie had a band of paleness around her hips and another at her breasts. Her nipples were dark, and the triangle at her thighs was as black as the hair on her head. Sloan's manhood rose strong and proud from a dark nest, his chest was furred and his arms and legs were sprinkled with the same dark hair.

Maggie swallowed. "You're a beautiful man," she whispered.

He took a step and pulled her up against himself, uniting her smaller form with his. Her rigid little nipples burning his chest, the way her firm behind felt in his hands, her smooth, warm flesh branding him—all of her sweet-smelling femaleness was making him half-crazed with desire.

His kiss was wildly possessive, arousingly demanding. "I love you," he rasped. "I love you, Maggie."

She couldn't stop herself. Her feelings welled up and erupted in a gasped, "I love you, too."

She felt herself being lifted, and her legs automatically went around his hips. Then he was inside her, penetrating the core of her desire, filling her. He put his back against the cottonwood and easily held her, and staring into her eyes, he began to move, seductively, deliciously.

Maggie could hardly breathe. No sexual fantasy could ever have surpassed the eroticism of what they were doing. His thrusts were slow but forceful, reaching that deep, private flame within her. She couldn't stop staring into his eyes, and saw deep within them excitement, desire, and the unmistakable glow of masculine domination.

She couldn't dispute it. Sloan was controlling them both, by pure physical strength, by the proficiency of his body. Her hands were locked together behind his neck, her lips parted, her expression fervent.

"You're hot," he whispered. "Hot and tight."

"You make me hot."

Maggie could have sworn that the blue of his eyes got suddenly darker with her admission. He slowly slid down the tree until he was sitting on the grass and she was straddling his lap. Her waiting lips received a passionate kiss, and she pressed into him, kissing him back with all the fire in her soul. His hand moved in between them, and he found the center of her need and began a circling caress.

Her senses leaped with new abandonment, and subtly, the control of their lovemaking shifted from him to her. Breathing hard, she lifted and fell, pleasuring him, pleasuring herself. His chest expanded with gulping breaths. The drive to reach fulfillment gripped Maggie, and she lost all sense of everything but Sloan and her feelings for him.

"Love me," she panted. "Love me."

"I do, baby. I love you. I love you."

Neatly, then, he tipped her over, and she found herself on her back, staring up into blue eyes that were almost hard with emotion. There was little gentleness in the final ride, but its tone was set by both of them. The tempo was increasingly harder and faster, until the heat in Maggie gathered into a compact fist and then exploded into spinning, whirling shards of her soul. She cried out once, then again, and ended in a sobbing moan, only vaguely aware that Sloan, too, had been vocal in his release.

Then they were quiet and still. Maggie's eyes were closed and tears seeped from between her lashes, an aftermath of so much emotion. Her body was replete with satisfaction, and for a few minutes even her mind maintained a beautiful serenity.

Sloan moved first, raising his head to look at her. He smiled, a soft, slow smile that reached his eyes and created a special shine. "My own love," he said, a husky declaration of their new status. If it was a touch proprietary, he couldn't help it. He loved Maggie Holloway madly, and he knew, as he'd told her, that he had fallen in love with her ten years ago. It seemed nothing short of a miracle to him that fate had brought them together again after so many years. There was irony in that fate being nothing but a herd of sheep, but he was too wise to point that out to Maggie now. Maybe someday, but not now.

Maggie turned her head, eluding the loving light in his eyes. It surprised Sloan, and some of the warmth fled his system. "Don't turn away from me," he pleaded softly.

She looked at him again, and her expression wasn't unkind. But the tempest was back in her soul, and she couldn't pretend it wasn't. So they loved each other. Love wasn't the end-all to problems. Love didn't automatically smooth a decidedly rocky path for two people, if that's what they were trodding on. And they were. She and Sloan could talk about love for days, weeks, and they would still have the same hurdles to overcome.

Yet she couldn't control her libido with Sloan, and he proved it again with a long, smoldering kiss. She couldn't believe it, but her heart actually began racing again. Unnerved, she tore her mouth from his. "Let me get up," she whispered.

His voice was heavy, thickening with desire again. "I could make love to you for hours, Maggie."

"No," she gasped. "Please . . . let me up."

Sloan studied her, then sighed and rolled away. Maggie jumped up and ran for the pond. Her skin was hot and sweaty, and she waded into the water and ducked beneath it, grateful for its coolness. She watched Sloan follow her in, and she formed a smile for him, unable to give him less.

The water wasn't deep, but he dove beneath the surface and came up laughing. "Ah, that's great." He looked around, then back to Maggie. "I'll bet you swam here a lot as a kid."

Maggie was on her knees, and the water lapped just under her chin. "Every chance I got," she admitted. "I skinny-dipped."

His eyes narrowed on her thoughtfully, as if he were seeing the younger Maggie. "With your long hair dripping water on your face, like now. Maggie, you're a beautiful sight. I wish you could see yourself through my eyes."

She laughed self-consciously and looked away from the blatant admiration on his face. "What am I going to do with you?" she said, making a stab at teasing, although there was a poignant truth in her voice.

Sloan walked towards her. Standing, the water only reached his navel, and droplets glistened in his hair and on his skin. "You could marry me," he said quietly, reaching for her and drawing her up by a grasp of her shoulders.

It didn't surprise her. In fact, she accepted the offhanded proposal with an air of resignation. Deep down she'd known it was coming, sooner or later.

They stared directly into each other's eyes, naked, dripping water, his hands gripping her upper arms. "Maggie, I'm asking—"

"I know what you're asking. But I'm sorry. I don't have an answer right on the tip of my tongue."

He shook her slightly. "You love me."

"I . . ."

"You do! You even said you did."

Sighing, Maggie looked away. "I need some time."

"For what?"

Her head jerked around. "For what! Sloan, all my plans for the ranch—just what do you think I should do with them? Toss them out the window? I've put a lot of money and hard work into this place. I'm not ready to chuck everything."

He seemed to stall, and Maggie knew then that she'd had good reason to worry about a future together. Sloan's rugged individualism contained just enough overconfidence that recognition of their "problem", which he'd admitted, didn't mean he'd given it any real credence. His wife would live on his ranch, end of subject.

But he was beginning to understand: Maggie could see it in his eyes. And she also heard it in his voice when he said, "My God, we can't let that keep us apart. We can't, Maggie."

"I'm eager to hear how you intend preventing it."

He looked stunned, and Maggie saw that at long last he grasped the full picture. His first reaction then was physical. He grabbed her in a fierce embrace, and the contact of their wet bare skin sent a fiery jolt through Maggie. He began kissing her, his mouth roaming over her face. "We can't let this happen," he groaned hoarsely. "We can't. Not now. Not when we're so close to . . . Oh, Maggie . . ."

There was frustration in the way his hands moved over her. Maggie felt them sweep down her back, then up again with an unnatural quiver. Her heart ached for him, and the unselfish empathy made her realize just how much she did love him. Maybe they were in this together much more than she'd known, she thought, recalling how her previous attempts to unsnarl the situation had seemed so solitary.

And how easily, how effortlessly he stimulated desire within her again. Maggie wasn't even slightly convinced they could find a solution to what seemed like an insurmountable dilemma, but she couldn't prevent her blood from racing when she was in his arms. Especially in their present state, nude, standing in waist-deep water that was cool and silky on her legs.

She turned her face, seeking his lips, and their kiss was rough, needful, agitated. His hands went below the water line to her hips, and he drew their lower bodies tightly together. He was hard and ready, and he moved against her while his tongue probed her mouth.

Then he raised his head and looked at her with ravaged eyes. "I want you. I want you now and for the rest of our lives."

"How?" she whispered, deeply shaken. "How are we to resolve...?"

He gave his head a small shake. "Right now I don't know. But we'll find a way, that I promise you." He bent then and scooped her up and out of the water, and in three long strides had gained the bank of the pond.

Sloan laid her down on the grass beneath the cottonwood. He picked up his shirt and began drying her with it. He was gentle again, patting moisture from her breasts, her thighs, her feet.

Maggie sat up and tugged the shirt out of his hands. Her eyes were warm and filled with emotion while she dried him. Her movements over his throat and chest were caressing, and when she brought the shirt downward, she saw a hot light flash on in his eyes. Her gaze dropped, and she stopped to look, creating a provocative pause. Then she sent an admiring glance to his face, smiled softly and boldly proceeded with the shirt-towel.

She dried him much more than he needed, but it was such a delight to touch him intimately. When she finally stopped, his breathing was irregular and his expression dark with desire.

She held up the shirt, and he took it and tossed it away. They moved toward one another, as if drawn by a mystical force.

They stayed at the pond all afternoon, making love, swimming, talking. When the sun was low in the western sky they dressed and started the ride back.

"I know you love this place," Sloan said after a few minutes.

Maggie held Rebel's reins loosely. Things were strangely right and disturbing, both at the same time. She'd never felt more loved in her life, nor had she ever experienced a day like today. Maybe she and Sloan were still on a rocky path, but they were on it together, she now knew.

"Yes." She didn't have to expand on the reply to Sloan's comment. A simple yes said it all.

Sloan's hat shadowed his eyes, but Maggie felt their impact. "One of us would have to make a major concession," he said quietly.

She nodded and agreed with another, "Yes."

"We could still operate both ranches."

"But we could only live on one," Maggie murmured.

"Not necessarily."

Her eyes widened. "Live on both?"

"It's an option, isn't it?"

"I suppose it is," she replied thoughtfully. "One that never occurred to me, to be honest."

Sloan directed his horse close enough to Maggie's to touch her arm. "Let's think about it, all right?"

Would she think of anything else? Live on both ranches? Maintain two homes? My Lord, was it even possible?

Something inside Maggie rejoiced for a moment, but her natural compulsion to plan ahead suddenly gave her a sting. Two homes might work for a while, but not indefinitely. If they had children—which was a very important part of marriage to her—it wouldn't be in their best interests to commute back and forth between Montana and Wyoming.

And she knew Sloan wanted children, too. That had been, according to what he'd told her about his first marriage, one of its breaking points, his desire for children and his ex-wife's refusal.

Maggie sighed soulfully. It wasn't going to be easy.

But then, was anything worth having ever easy?

There had to be an answer.

Ten

When Maggie and Sloan were coming up on the ranch buildings, he grinned at her. "I'd be glad to stay for dinner, if someone should happen to be wondering."

Maggie's laughter rang out. It really had been the most incredible afternoon, and whatever else might be in store for them, the hours at the pond would always remain beautiful and special. "You're invited," she declared. "I'm not promising a feast, however."

"A feast isn't even remotely necessary," Sloan said, laughing. "But I am hungry. How about you?"

"I'm sure I can scare up something, and yes, I'm hungry, too."

They were riding side-by-side beneath a glorious pink-streaked sunset. The buildings were shadowed rectangles in the glowing evening light, and there was such peace in the scene, Maggie had to blink back a tear. She did love this old place. Passionately, she realized again, then shied away from the thought. Somehow she had slid into a commitment with

Sloan, and a part of her was profoundly happy about it while another part was equally saddened.

She was still torn, pulled in two directions, and even Sloan's determination to overcome the situation was only mildly comforting.

Releasing a small private sigh, Maggie smiled at her companion. At least they'd gotten past the sheep problem and she felt finally cleansed of that old prejudice. It seemed foolish now, and she had no intention of reminding Sloan of their many battles and bitter words about it.

The first building they reached was the barn. As they rode around to the front of it Maggie approvingly noted Les's efforts of the day. One entire end of the structure had been scraped. With both of them working on it, it should be ready for painting in another few days.

After that they would tackle the exterior of the house, which would pretty much wind up the renovations Maggie had planned. She already had plans beyond structural repairs, however. The fields could all be improved with fertilizer and some reseeding, and there were several that Maggie wanted to seed with alfalfa hay. In her grandfather's day, the ranch had raised wonderful hay crops, enough to see the cattle through the worst winter. It was a part of Maggie's overall plan to eventually grow all of her own winter feed, just as Lyle Holloway had.

Sloan dismounted first and went to help Maggie down. She threw her right leg over the front of the saddle and slid into Sloan's waiting arms. He held her for a moment, then kissed her. "I'm a happy man, Maggie," he said softly.

She smiled wistfully, wishing it was as simple for her. Why wasn't it? Why couldn't she rid herself of the doubts continuing to plague her? She did love Sloan; she was beyond denying it. But so much of her was tied to the ranch—so very much of her.

Rising on tiptoe, she kissed his lips again. "Let's unsaddle and go—" She stopped abruptly, dropping back and peering around Sloan. On her toes she'd been able to see the house over Sloan's shoulder, and there were lights on. "Sloan, someone must be in the house."

"What?" He turned. "There's a strange car—No, wait. Maggie, it's your dad's car."

"Oh, it couldn't be. Dad and Mother aren't due for almost a week." Maggie squinted at the dark sedan parked beside the house. She'd thought Mr. Jamison, the rancher who owned the Labradors, might have come by. But he wouldn't be in the house, and besides, there really was no doubt as to whose car she was looking at. "It is Dad's car," she said, suddenly choked with a fearful premonition.

But no, she was being silly. Bert's and Sarah's itinerary must have changed since she last talked to them. There was no point in getting worried just because they had arrived a week early. They were here for a visit, that's all, just a visit.

Maggie turned to Rebel and, flipping up the stirrup, reached for the horse's cinch belt. Sloan laid a hand on her shoulder. "Go on up to the house and see your folks, honey. I'll take care of the horses."

"No...I..." She glanced at Sloan's face and knew he couldn't possibly understand any show of reluctance to face her parents. Forcing herself to calm down, Maggie nodded her acceptance. "All right, thank you."

"I'll stop at the house before I leave."

"What about dinner?"

He smiled and gently touched her cheek. "We'll skip it for tonight. You'll want to spend your folks's first evening home with them."

"But you said you were hungry."

"I won't starve before I get home. Go on, honey. They're probably anxious to see you."

Maggie looked back at the house again. "Les probably told them I was out riding." She was putting it off, she knew, and wished her stomach would stop turning over. It was no doubt a ludicrous worry, just her imagination working overtime. But Bert had been on such a tight schedule all summer, and his arriving almost a week early seemed ominous.

She felt Sloan's hands on her, sliding down her back to her waist, and she faced him with a tremulous smile. He was so utterly dear to her, she acknowledged in a burst of love. How could she have fought so diligently against this feeling the way she had? The problem of two separate ranches surely had been faced by other couples; it couldn't be uniquely theirs.

Her hands slipped up around his neck and she pressed into his firm, warm body. They had made love so completely that afternoon that it surprised Maggie to feel desire again. Perhaps it would always be so, that tingling liquidity at contact with Sloan.

He was more than willing to hold and kiss her, but he sensed something amiss in Maggie's embrace. He could feel tension in her body, and when their lips separated he asked, "What's wrong, Maggie?"

"Why do you think something's wrong?" she returned, her heart pounding from the sexual excitement of their kiss.

His eyes held hers. "Nothing's wrong? You're sure?"

Laughing shakily, Maggie pulled away. "Nothing's wrong," she lied. Her anxiety had too many facets, making an explanation nearly impossible. Sloan already knew the portion of it that involved him. But Maggie suspected that while he understood it, he didn't see it as insurmountable. As for the portion involving her parents, even she doubted its validity. How would she explain it to Sloan? Besides, loyalty to her father, despite knowing him well enough to worry about his motives, precluded discussing her fears with anyone, even Sloan.

"I'll see you later," Maggie threw over her shoulder as she started for the house. Sloan watched her go with an uneasy expression. She was acting like she wasn't very thrilled that Bert and Sarah were there, and Sloan couldn't figure out why. Frowning, he turned to the horses and the task of un-saddling them.

Maggie walked without haste, her gaze on the lighted windows of the house. She saw her mother in the kitchen window, and then her father pass by. Sarah turned and said something, then Bert came into view again. He raked his fingers through his still thick, graying dark hair, and as Maggie got closer, she could see Bert's agitation.

Her stomach churned sickishly; Bert looked neither happy nor content.

Reaching the back door, Maggie took a deep breath, put a big smile on her face and opened it. "Well, my goodness, look who's here!" she exclaimed brightly.

"Maggie!" Sarah came forward and mother and daughter exchanged a sincerely affectionate hug.

Maggie had always thought of her mother as a beautiful woman. Sarah was tall and straight, with a dignified bearing. She had soft blue-gray eyes and light golden-brown hair, a color that camouflaged the few gray strands very well. Sarah had always dressed stylishly and was wearing a smart dusty-rose skirt and blouse, topped by a pretty white apron.

"Mother, you look wonderful. As usual," Maggie proclaimed.

"Thank you, dear. You look wonderful, too. So tan. Doesn't she look marvelous, Bert?"

Maggie turned to her father. Bert Holloway smiled and held out his arms. "Give your old dad a hug."

"It's good to see you, Dad," Maggie murmured as she wrapped her arms around her father. When she stepped back, she took her hat off and hung it on a hook by the door. Then she smiled at both parents. "What time did you get here?"

"Around two," Bert replied.

"Dinner is almost ready," Sarah announced. "I hope you're hungry. I made fried chicken, milk gravy and mashed potatoes, your favorite meal, Maggie."

"Yes, it is. Thank you, Mother." Maggie looked from one parent to the other. "Well, it's certainly good to see you both. I'm dying to hear all about the campaign. I'll bet you have dozens of good stories to tell, Dad."

Bert cleared his throat and glanced at Sarah. Maggie caught the exchange and shrank inwardly. All was not well. It was in the air, behind Bert's dark eyes, in the line of Sarah's lips. "I'll set the table," Maggie announced briskly, denying what she'd just seen.

"It's already set, dear. In the dining room," Sarah murmured, and turned to stir something simmering in a pot on the stove.

"Oh. In that case, I'll go and wash up." Wiping her sweaty palms on her jeans, Maggie started from the kitchen. "I'll only be a few minutes," she mumbled.

Maggie took the stairs two at a time and ran to her bedroom. She was trembling, and she sat on the edge of the bed, hugging herself. The entire day had been emotionally jarring, and too many jolts to her nervous system had left her feeling at loose ends and vulnerable.

She closed her eyes, and after a few moments of blessed oblivion, mentally berated herself. The afternoon with Sloan had something to do with her anxiety, and she shouldn't be actively looking for trouble from her parents. She was getting carried away again; neither Bert nor Sarah had given her any real reason to be so destroyed. All she'd done was pick up some restless vibes in the kitchen, and there could be a perfectly logical explanation for that.

Give Dad and Mother a chance, Maggie told herself with rapidly developing guilt. She really was glad to see them, and she should make them feel welcome, not spend the evening anticipating problems.

Somewhat calmer, Maggie got to her feet, gathered up clean clothes and headed for the bathroom. She was in the shower when she remembered that Sloan was going to stop at the house before he left. "Oh, God," she moaned, and covered her face with her hands while the shower spray pelted her back. Why had everything happened today? She was on edge, keyed up, and even the thought of seeing Sloan again was nerve-wracking.

Was this what love did to a person? Love for the ranch, love for her parents, love for Sloan—dammit, why was she tied in such knots over an emotion that *should* bring happiness?

Angrily, Maggie slammed the shower level to Off. The anger was directed at herself. She wasn't blaming anyone else for her emotional quandary, she couldn't. She'd lived as a responsible adult for too many years to start blaming other people for any dissatisfaction she might be feeling.

The thing to do, she decided firmly as she dried off and dressed, was to face her parents maturely. Whatever was bothering them wasn't going to disappear because she tried to elude it. As for Sloan—well, maybe he was right. If two people were truly in love, most problems could be worked out.

When Maggie descended the stairs ten minutes later, she heard Sloan's voice, along with her parents'. They were all in the kitchen, chatting like old friends. At the door, Maggie saw that Bert and Sloan were seated at the table, each with a glass of beer, and Sarah was hovering between stove and sink, putting the finishing touches to dinner.

"Oh, Maggie," Sarah smiled. "I invited Sloan to stay for dinner, but he said no. Maybe you can convince him. Tell him that I'm really a very good cook, dear."

Everyone laughed, although Maggie's contribution wasn't all that hearty. The truth was, she preferred Sloan not to stay. It was much better for all concerned if she and the older Holloways cleared the air, and Maggie became even more determined to do so when she looked at her father and realized again that something was wrong in his world.

"Sloan has other plans for tonight, Mother," Maggie said quietly, and at the surprise in Sloan's eyes, she sent him a silent message.

He got the drift. "That's right, Sarah. I thank you for your gracious invitation, and I most certainly will take a rain check, if you don't mind. But I really do have to be going." He finished off his glass of beer and stood up. "Bert, it's been great seeing you again."

Bert rose, and the two men shook hands. "Drop in anytime," Bert declared, and another icy finger licked at Maggie's insides.

"I'll walk you out to your truck," she said in a strange, hoarse voice, and saw Sloan's eyes narrow curiously.

Sarah called a pleasant, "Good night, Sloan" as they walked out of the house. The second the door was closed and they were alone, Sloan took Maggie by the arm.

"What the hell's going on, Maggie?"

It had grown dark. Maggie shivered, although the night air was still warm. "Are you going to tell me?" Sloan persisted. They stopped beside his pickup.

"No." Realizing how abrupt she'd sounded, Maggie sighed. "Sloan, there's nothing to tell, not until I talk to Dad and Mother."

"Then tell me what you're worried about. Maggie, the minute you saw your folks' car you got upset."

"It just surprised me. I didn't expect them for a while yet. Look, I'm not even sure I have a legitimate worry. If I do...well, you and everyone else will know all about it very soon."

Sloan sucked in a sharp breath of comprehension. "The ranch. You're worried about the ranch. I thought you bought it."

"I did," Maggie replied wearily. "Sloan, you'd have to know a lot more than you do about my family to understand.'' She glanced at the house. "I better go in. Mother has dinner ready.''

He put his hands on her shoulders and urged her forward. "Would you call me later?''

Sighing again, Maggie locked her arms around his waist and put her head on his chest. "I don't know. Don't make me promise. I don't know how the evening will go.''

His lips caressed her hair. "I love you,'' he whispered. "Whatever else happens, will you hang on to that?''

"Yes, I'll hang on to that,'' she replied softly, surprising herself by how true that was. Sloan's love was already incredibly important to her, a haven. His arms felt like a safe harbor, and she snuggled deeper into them.

He grabbed a labored breath. "Do you know how you affect me? At your slightest touch I want you. Holding you like this is torture when I know we can't do anything.''

She tilted her head back and smiled up at him. She agreed one hundred percent with that observation, but she couldn't resist a bit of teasing. "Didn't we *do* enough today?''

He shook his head slowly and grinned. "Never. You make my blood boil, Maggie.''

On tiptoe, she whispered against his lips, "And you make mine steam. Kiss me, then I've got to go in.''

They both tried to keep the kiss cool, but it wasn't possible, and they ended up gasping for air. When Sloan began to work the blue print skirt up that she'd put on with a red blouse for dinner, Maggie backed away. "Good night,'' she said breathlessly.

"Good night, and if you need to talk to me later on, just call.''

"I will, thanks.'' Maggie ran for the house and heard Sloan's pickup motor start just as she went through the back door.

Sarah was waiting in the kitchen. "Dinner's on the table. Your father is already in the dining room.''

"Sorry I held you up.''

"Oh, that's quite all right. Sloan Prescott is certainly a nice-looking man, isn't he?" Sarah smiled all the way to the dining room.

"Yes, he's very nice-looking," Maggie agreed, taking the side seat of the dining table. Bert occupied the head of the table and Sarah took her place at its foot. They all bowed their heads while Bert said a brief prayer of thanks.

"Well," Sarah said cheerily. "Isn't this nice? Being together again, I mean?" She passed the platter of chicken to Maggie, while Bert dug into the bowl of mashed potatoes.

"Very nice, Mother," Maggie concurred.

Comments on the food took up time while they filled their plates, and then Maggie couldn't keep silent another second. She looked at her father. "You got here early enough today to look around, Dad. What do you think of the place now?"

Bert's smile was broad and generous and only a touch nervous. "It looks great, Maggie, just great. You've got it in great shape. Great-looking cattle, too."

He'd used too many "greats". He was trying too hard. The icy fingers clutching Maggie's spine pinched a little tighter, and it took monumental effort to sound only interested in the topic at hand. "Yes, aren't they? Did you see the Thoroughbred mares?"

Sarah jumped in with, "Maggie, they're wonderful. You'll have beautiful foals from those mares and Rebel."

Maggie tried a bite of chicken breast and noticed the tremor in her hands. The chicken was delicious, which she'd expected. No one prepared chicken better than her mother did, but as excellent as the food was, Maggie's stomach wasn't quite up to eating. She put her fork down on her plate and looked at Bert again. She had to hear it, whatever "it" was. "How's the campaign going, Dad?"

Bert went on eating, chewing slowly, taking a drink from his water glass. Maggie glanced at her mother and saw an expectant expression on her face. Whatever had to be said, Sarah was predictably leaving it to her husband. "Dad?" Maggie urged.

"Well, honey, it's like this. I dropped out of the race."

For a frozen beat in time, Maggie didn't move a muscle. Her mouth felt oddly numb and lifeless. She had to tell herself not to rush to conclusions. Dropping out of the race didn't necessarily mean Bert wanted the ranch again.

The silence was deafening, and then Maggie managed a reasonably normal, "Can you do that? I mean, aren't you committed to see it through?"

"I was running as an independent, Maggie."

"Well, yes, but you have . . . or, had . . . quite a lot of people working with you. What about them?"

"Aw, they don't care. Do they, Sarah? They understand that my heart just isn't in it anymore."

Maggie swallowed the harsh, dry lump in her throat. "May I ask why not?"

"Your father is tired, Maggie," Sarah said softly.

Bert started eating again, and Maggie watched him while a slow-burning fury began to sear her brain. "Tired" wasn't it at all, she knew. Bert was a healthy, robust man. The only way "tired" came into the picture was that Bert had gotten tired of the game. For God knew what reason, the glamour of politics had worn off. And, like Jake Barnett had maintained, Bert had "skedaddled" for home.

Except this was no longer his home. It was *hers*!

A glaze of rage made the dining room swim in a sea of red for Maggie. She had never been so angry in her life. She had worked and sweated and spent her money. She had long-term plans and goals. Bert couldn't have the ranch! It was hers, dammit, hers!

Her hands clenched into fists on her lap beneath the tablecloth. "What are your plans, then, Dad?" she asked, and even she heard the ice in her voice.

Bert looked up, total surprise on his face. "Plans?"

Sarah interceded again. "We realize how this might seem to you, Maggie, but..."

"Seem, Mother? *Seem?*"

"Don't you take that tone with your mother, young woman," Bert said, throwing down his napkin.

This could erupt into a fight, Maggie saw. Bert never had accepted censure of anything he'd ever done. And the way she felt now, the things she was capable of saying would be worse than disapproving; they would be brutally honest and condemning.

Only through intense concentration were Maggie's hands relatively steady as she folded her napkin and laid it on the table. "Please excuse me, Mother. I think it's best if I leave for a while."

"No, wait!" Sarah cried, getting up when Maggie did. "Please, Maggie, we can talk this out. Bert, stop her."

"How?" Bert got to his feet, but it was plain that he didn't know what to do. Maggie looked from parent to parent, and nearly choked on the rage in her soul. She started to speak, to hurl something bitter at them, but she stopped herself and whirled around, leaving the dining room in a flurry of flying skirt and hair.

She tried to think. Her car keys were in her purse, which was upstairs in her room. She knew she had no choice but to get out of the house. If she stayed...

No, she wouldn't think about that. Releasing her bitterness would do nothing except cause an unmendable breach in the family.

Maggie ran up the stairs, grabbed her purse and ran back down to the first floor. She could hear Bert's and Sarah's voices in the dining room, Sarah's soft, as always, Bert's blustering. Maggie didn't stop to listen, but hurried through the kitchen and out the back door.

Her heart was beating wildly and her eyes stinging with threatening tears. *I should have known, I should have known*, echoed through her head.

She climbed into her car and, with trembling hands, fit the key into the ignition.

Eleven

Maggie had no destination in mind. But knowing how disturbed she was, she drove slowly, sticking to back roads with little or no traffic. It was a warm night with a bright quarter-moon, a beautiful night, but velvety air and a spectacular sky did nothing to diminish the storm in Maggie's soul.

Her anger alternated with self-castigation. She should have known! She should have relied on Bert's mercurial history. He had never stayed with either a vocation or an avocation for any length of time. In her own fervency for the ranch, she had arrogantly sidestepped that fact. And it *was* a fact, a hard, cruel fact, which was one of the things she could have cut her parents to ribbons with.

She could have pointed out to Sarah that love was grand, but maybe a wife's responsibility went a little further than constant yeses to a man's whims.

She could have stood up and declared, "You are both welcome to stay here, but you will have no say in the ranch's operation. It is mine now. It is repaired and clean and functioning again. Through me, Dad. Because of me, Mother.''

Maggie's vision blurred with tears and she pulled over to the side of the road. Digging for a tissue in her purse she sobbed quietly. She hated the empty futility gripping her, but that's how she felt, helpless, powerless.

Legally the ranch was hers. George Shipley had drawn up a good contract, and Maggie had already made two payments on it. But, as had previously occurred to her, legality had little to do with how one might handle a family problem.

"Oh, damn, damn, damn," Maggie whispered, weakened again by the enormity of her situation. Even angry at them, she loved her parents. And she certainly would never do anything to bring a family problem to public attention. Which pretty much defeated any clout legality might have had in straightening out the nightmare.

Maggie put the car in gear again and pulled back onto the road. She couldn't drive around all night, but neither was she ready to go back to the ranch. Her anger was a little more subdued now, but still too close to the surface to risk facing Bert again tonight. She well knew his volatile personality and how defensive he was about his conduct. If she returned now, they were sure to get into an argument.

In some ways her father was terribly insensitive, Maggie thought. How cavalier he'd been about the people who'd been working on the campaign with him. But on second thought, Maggie had to admit that Bert had no enemies that she knew of. People always forgave him, for some crazy reason.

Then there was Sarah's point of view. Maggie knew that in her mother's eyes, Robert Holloway never needed forgiveness, because he never did anything really wrong. His impulsiveness actually seemed to be endearing to her, and when he was fractious, Sarah soothed him with soft words. She had never, to Maggie's knowledge, ever apologized to anyone for her husband. She loved him and saw only perfection in him.

Maggie chewed her bottom lip and frowned at the road ahead. Her parents love for each other was unquestionable. When Maggie was old enough for serious conversation on the subject of men and women, Sarah had confided quite openly that she and Bert had a wonderful sex life, and that their physical communion, along with their emotional love, had made them an extremely happy couple.

For the first time Maggie really understood her mother's confidence that day. She felt so much of the same thing with Sloan, both a physical and an emotional attachment, that she understood her parents' love much better. Not that Maggie felt she could ever be as subservient as Sarah. Maggie had too much of her father—and her grandfather—in her to follow anyone blindly, even a man she truly loved. She knew she'd inherited Bert's volatile temper, but, thank God, she'd also inherited some of her mother's gentle avoid-trouble-wherever-possible nature. Which was probably the only reason she hadn't exploded at the dinner table tonight.

Nevertheless, in assessing her parents, Maggie knew that her problem was with her father, not Sarah. No doubt Bert had just up and declared, "We're going home, Sarah," and without even asking why, Sarah had started packing. In summation, Maggie knew that appealing to her mother would do absolutely no good. She must deal with Bert on the subject of the ranch.

At that conclusion, Maggie sighed long and dejectedly. Dealing with Bert was like playing the old shell game. Now you see it, now you don't.

After another few miles of lamenting her plight, Maggie's thoughts turned to Sloan. He knew very little about her father, and had even told her how much he liked Bert. Well, Bert was a likable fellow. He had oodles of friends, which was probably what had gotten him into state politics in the first place. Oddly enough, Maggie felt that those same friends would undoubtedly rally around and support Bert's decision to quit. He had that kind of charisma.

Earlier tonight Maggie had avoided discussing her fears for the ranch with Sloan because of family loyalty. But now she was thinking that her loyalty might be just a mite misplaced. Who better to discuss her worries with than the man she loved? Who had more of a right to learn of a family's idiosyncrasies than a man who was planning to be a part of it through marriage?

"Lord," Maggie mumbled, wondering just how to explain Bert Holloway so Sloan would understand. It occurred to her that she'd never tried to explain her father to anyone before. In that respect she was like Sarah, but unlike Sarah, Maggie had gotten into plenty of brouhahas with Bert.

As a teenager she'd rebelled at unreasonableness. Anyone's unreasonableness, and she'd seen her father as unreasonable many times. Her grandfather had often taken her side in an issue, her mother had stayed neutral, and Bert and Maggie had sometimes gone at it tooth and nail. The anger had never lasted beyond the last hot word, thank goodness, simply because neither of them had ever held grudges.

But if she and Sloan were going anywhere, and after today Maggie felt they were, it was time he heard something in the way of Holloway history.

The decision made Maggie feel somewhat better, and she turned the car south. Sloan had said to call him if she needed to talk, so her visit shouldn't be that much of a surprise.

Maggie shook her head. Her visit *would* be a surprise. She'd never been back to Sloan's place after that meeting about the grazing lease, and there was no reason for him to expect her to just drop in tonight. He'd probably be plenty surprised.

* * *

Sloan hung up the phone, then left the study and walked out the front door to the porch. He'd been uneasy all evening about Maggie, and had finally said to hell with that foolishness and given her a call. Only she wasn't there.

Sarah Holloway had answered the phone and Sloan had asked for Maggie right away.

"I'm sorry, Sloan. She isn't here."

He'd detected strain in Sarah's voice. "Where is she, Sarah?"

"I—I wish I knew. She took her car. Sloan, this isn't your problem, but we had a, well, I suppose one could call it a little falling out. Nothing serious, mind you. But Maggie was quite upset when she left."

"This *is* my problem, Sarah. I'm in love with your daughter and I've asked her to marry me."

"You have? Well, for heaven's sake. I wish Maggie or you had said something."

"I was leaving that up to Maggie. Is Bert handy?"

"He's out talking to Les right now. Should I have him call you back?"

"No, I guess that's not necessary. When Maggie shows up, though, would you ask her to call me right away?"

"Yes, of course. Well, it sounds like congratulations are in order. I have a feeling that Bert will be very pleased."

"Not yet, Sarah. Maggie hasn't said yes yet."

Sloan leaned against a porch post and stared across a dark field to the highway. The lights of passing cars flashed intermittently but the road was far enough away from the house that very little highway sound reached the premises.

He thought of what he'd told Sarah, "Maggie hasn't said yes yet." It was true. Maggie *hadn't* said yes. Her reluctance to make that final commitment was because of the Holloway ranch. With Bert and Sarah back, perhaps wanting the ranch again . . . ?

Sloan stopped himself from putting the idea into a concrete thought. It was damned unfair of him to hope that the Holloways were back for good. After all the work, time, money and emotion Maggie had put into the place, how could he even favorably contemplate such a thing?

Still, a small grin touched his lips. It would solve everything!

And he wouldn't be human if he didn't feel some jubilation about the possibility.

Pacing the length of the porch, Sloan sobered and wondered where Maggie had gone. And how serious had that "little falling out" been? Maybe he better cut the adolescent elation until he found out just what was going on in the Holloway family, he decided. If he had even the slightest idea where to start, he'd go looking for Maggie.

The telephone jangled, and Sloan frowned at the interruption, then yanked the screen door open and went inside to answer it. "Sloan Prescott here," he announced.

"Sloan, this is Bert Holloway. Sarah just told me you called. What's this about you and Maggie?"

There was acceptance, approval and humor in Bert's voice, and Sloan settled into a chair with a grin. "She hasn't said yes, Bert."

"Well, I'm betting she will. Seriously, Sloan, I couldn't be happier. Congratulations."

"Thanks, Bert. I'm a little concerned right now. Do you have any idea where she might have gone?"

"No, I don't. She's got a temper, Sloan, but I think you already know that." Bert chuckled, man-to-man. "We talked on the phone quite a bit in the past two months and she told her mother and me about a few of your run-ins over your sheep."

Sloan felt himself withdrawing from the camaraderie in Bert's voice. What he and Maggie had wasn't open for discussion, not with anyone. He liked Bert, and Sarah, too, but Maggie came first. "She had a right to be upset, Bert. Listen, I already mentioned it to Sarah, but when Maggie gets home, ask her to call me, all right?''

"Sure thing.''

After good-byes, Sloan stared at the phone reflectively. He didn't feel very elated anymore, he realized. He was getting damned worried. Apparently, whatever had taken place at the Holloway ranch hadn't affected Bert all that much. But Maggie was off God knew where, and maybe *very* affected. What was she doing, just driving around by herself? Or maybe she had a friend she could talk to.

Sloan got to his feet and started for the front door again. The house seemed confining tonight, and there was no way he could just sit and relax with Maggie upset and running around the countryside.

Just as he stepped out on the porch he saw the headlights of a car turn into his driveway. Sloan knew instantly who it was, and he breathed a silent prayer of thanks that Maggie had come to him. He went out to meet her, and stood at the edge of the driveway waiting for her.

Maggie saw Sloan standing there and brushed at the tears that suddenly formed. She stopped the car, turned off the key and the door opened before she could reach the handle.

Sloan pulled her into his arms. "Oh, baby," he said huskily, and the sympathetic tone of his voice was all it took for a complete breakdown. She sobbed on his shirt, and he rocked her and crooned to her until she got hold of herself.

Sniffling, she said hoarsely, "I'm sorry. I had no intention of crying on your shoulder.''

He tilted her chin and smiled down at her. "You can cry on my shoulder anytime you feel the need.''

"Do you have a handkerchief? I used the last of my tissues, I'm afraid.''

"Let's go inside. There are tissues all over the place.''

Maggie formed a feeble smile and let herself be led across the lawn and into the house. Sloan brought her to a first-floor bathroom and turned on the light. "Wash your face and blow your nose," he said gently. "I'll be in the study."

"Thank you." Maggie closed the bathroom door and spotted a box of tissues. She came out five minutes later. Her eyes were red and swollen, but she was much calmer. Unfamiliar with Sloan's house, she looked up and down the hallway, trying to get her bearings.

"In here, honey," Sloan called from a doorway.

"I couldn't remember," she murmured, walking toward him. He put his arm around her shoulders and brought her into the room and to the sofa.

"What can I get you? Coffee, tea, something stronger?"

Maggie nodded with a grim expression. "Something stronger, I think. Whatever you have on hand will be fine."

"A little brandy will probably do the trick." Sloan went to a cabinet and splashed brandy into two small snifters. He returned to Maggie, gave her one of the glasses, then sat down beside her.

"Thanks," she said absently and took a sip.

"Now, just what's so terrible?" he asked quietly.

Maggie stared down into her drink, then had to wipe her eyes again. She'd had no idea that seeing Sloan would make her feel so emotional, but she couldn't seem to maintain control. "I've got to stop this," she said with a weak, embarrassed laugh.

"No, you don't. You don't have to put up any kind of front with me, Maggie. If you feel like bawling, bawl. If you feel like screaming, go ahead and cut one loose. Just be yourself, honey. Whatever's inside, let it out."

She slumped back against the sofa and looked at him. "Do you remember the night we saw each other at Shannon's?"

"Yes, of course I do."

Maggie brushed her hair back from her face with a weary gesture. How could he not remember it after what she'd said to him? "Yes, I'm sure you do. Anyway, I ran into a lot of old friends that night, friends of the family. One of them, Jake Barnett, said something to me that started me worrying.''

"I know Jake. What'd he say?"

Maggie took a sip of brandy. "That Dad would be through with politics and back to the ranch before Labor Day."

"Is that what happened?" Sloan asked softly, already positive of it, but not sure it would be wise to let Maggie know that he'd figured it out at this point. She obviously needed to talk, and he was deeply moved and grateful that she'd come to him.

"Yes, that's exactly what happened. He quit the race, Sloan. Just like that, without a thought for anyone else, he simply dropped out." Maggie raised the glass to her lips for another sip. "I knew he was capable of doing it and it still shocked the hell out of me."

"I'm sure it did," Sloan murmured. He could see bitterness and resentment and frustration in Maggie's eyes, and he wondered how he could have been even slightly jubilant over something that was hurting her so badly.

But Sloan had another concern, too. He wanted to marry Maggie, which meant that Bert and Sarah would be his in-laws. Family members didn't always see eye to eye, but they cared for each other anyway. Maggie was lucky to still have her parents, and Sloan knew that as earthshaking as this trouble seemed to Maggie, it would eventually blow over. Somehow, some way, this breach would heal, and when it was over, the Holloways would be united again. Sloan didn't want to do something now to put himself on the outside of that circle.

What he had to do was console Maggie and soothe some pretty battered emotions, and, at the same time, encourage her to understand her parents. Or, more accurately, her father.

The first step was letting her talk out her anger.

"So Bert said he wants the ranch back?" Sloan asked, purposely feeding Maggie's rage.

It worked. She seemed to swell with emotion, then she jumped up and began to pace. "No," she declared heatedly. "He didn't say it right out, but he didn't have to. Mother says he's tired. Tired! He's tired, all right, tired of doing the same thing for more than a few weeks."

Maggie turned, and her eyes were burning coals in her face. "You don't know my father, Sloan. He's never stayed with anything for a normal length of time in his entire life. I'll never know how he managed to finish college and law school. It was probably only because he wanted to avoid the ranch at the time.

"The ranch. Dammit, he didn't want it, Sloan! He told me to do anything I wanted to with it."

Sloan sipped his brandy and remained silent. It was tough to sit still and watch Maggie's torment when what he wanted to do was hold her. She looked even smaller than she was in her misery, lost and frightened. But he knew she had to get this out of her system.

He almost weakened and went to her when he saw her wipe away another tear. "I wanted it," she said, her voice thick with emotion. "I've always wanted it."

Sloan nodded. "That must be when he offered to sell it to you."

"What?" Startled, Maggie came to an abrupt stop.

"When he realized how much you wanted the ranch. Isn't that when he offered to sell it to you?"

Maggie stared, then tipped her glass and finished her brandy. When she lowered the snifter, she said very quietly, "He never offered."

"Pardon?"

"I said, he didn't make the offer. I'm the one who suggested it."

"Oh." Sloan sat back, pondering the implications of Maggie having instigated the transaction.

"It really doesn't matter who suggested it," Maggie said defensively. "He agreed. So did Mother. They both said several times that they didn't want to ever live on the ranch again. I made very sure of that before I even brought up the matter."

"I see."

Maggie glared. "No, you don't see. You're thinking that I pushed them into it, aren't you?"

Sloan held up a hand. "Hey, don't get mad at me. I'm on your team." With a little reverse psychology in mind he declared offhandedly, "If you want my honest opinion, I think your father's behavior is juvenile, irresponsible and downright disgusting."

Maggie backed up two steps. "Well, I don't know if you should go that far. After all, Dad was born and raised on that ranch." She closed her eyes for a second. "Damn, what am I saying? He never liked the place, never! He neglected it, he sold the stock, he wasted money, he let the whole place go to seed! Why did he keep coming back to it when he didn't like it? You know, after every scheme he tried, he always came back to the ranch. Even when Granddad was alive, Dad would go off and try some new idea for a while. Then, when it failed, there he'd be."

"Your mother, too?"

Maggie shrugged. "Where Dad went, Mother went."

"And you? What about you?"

"Why, I stayed with Granddad, of course."

Sloan leaned forward. "Why of course, Maggie? Don't you think it's a little out of the ordinary for parents to repeatedly go off and leave their only child with her grandfather?"

Maggie's eyes snapped. "I *wanted* to stay!"

"Maybe when you were old enough to make that decision, yes. But what about when you were younger?"

"Sloan, that has nothing to do with what's going on today."

"I'm not so sure of that, honey. Maybe I'm completely off base here, but haven't you ever wondered why you're so attached to that place?"

"Have you ever wondered why you're so attached to this one?" Maggie hurled angrily.

Sloan nodded. "Yes, I have, as a matter of fact. It's because of my dad. After my mother died, Dad and I were all we had, and we were as close as any father and son could ever be. I told you about that."

Maggie turned away to collect herself. She'd been petty to attack Sloan's bond with his ranch. His situation had nothing to do with hers, and he was only trying to help. She was hurt, but lashing out at Sloan was inexcusable.

"I'm sorry," she said, facing him again. "I just feel so utterly helpless."

"Yes, I know you do. But you're not helpless, Maggie. You're the most un-helpless woman I've ever known. You have a problem, yes. But you have solutions, too."

"I do?"

"Come and sit down, honey." Sloan patted the sofa cushion beside him. Maggie slowly complied, and when she was seated, Sloan took her hands.

"First of all, you have me."

A slight wariness entered Maggie's eyes. "Sloan . . ."

The corner of his mouth turned up in a wry grin. "Don't you want me?"

The question was so point-blank, demanding a yes or no answer, and Maggie didn't want to deal with their relationship right now. "Let's not talk about us tonight," she pleaded. "The only thing I can think of is the ranch."

"It's all intermingled, Maggie. You, me, our ranches, your folks. Don't you see that? That's the first thing you should face, that you're not in this alone."

Her face grew very solemn. "Only to a degree, Sloan. I realized today that you don't see my affiliation with my ranch as a serious obstacle for us. You're not alone in that attitude, I might add. I think Dad and Mother look on it as some sort of trivial whim."

Sloan's gaze moved over her features. "Are you given to whimsy?"

"No, that's Dad's department," she replied bitterly. "Why did they agree to sell? Getting down to the central core of it, why did I think it would be permanent? Nothing ever was, not with Dad."

"It was with your grandfather, right?"

"Granddad was the most stable person I've ever known. Yes, his life had permanence and purpose."

"You loved him best, didn't you? Growing up, I mean. Your grandfather was the most important person to you, wasn't he?"

Maggie's face became flushed with emotion. "Yes, I loved him best. Why wouldn't I? He was the only one who loved…" She stopped, realizing what she'd just said. Sloan was still holding her hands, and she eased away from him and huddled in the corner of the sofa.

"The only one who loved you?" Sloan gently prodded.

She sent him a humiliated glance.

"Face it, honey. Take it out and face it."

Tears scalded her eyes and she covered them with her hands. Her voice was muffled and hoarse. "Mother and Dad only loved each other. They had no time for me."

Sloan closed his eyes against the pain he could see in her small frame. She was tough and courageous on the outside, and a small, hurt child on the inside. No wonder she wanted the ranch so badly. It was a symbol of Lyle Holloway, the only security she'd known as a youngster.

Maggie dropped her hands and inhaled deeply. "That's not entirely true," she amended. "Mother and Dad did love me, but they were so wrapped up in each other and in Dad's schemes, they often forgot I existed. Granddad was always there."

Her eyes softened. "I wish you could have known him. He was kind and funny and never too busy to answer my incessant questions."

Sloan smiled. "But he didn't like sheep."

Maggie smiled, too, a weak effort. "No, he didn't like sheep. But you have to consider his background. He was old enough to remember when there was real dissension between the two factions. And then, of course, he'd grown up on stories from an even older generation."

"Which he passed on to you." Sloan slid closer to her. "How do you feel about that now, Maggie?"

"About sheep?" Sighing, Maggie laid her head back and stared at the ceiling. Then she brought her eyes to Sloan and raised a hand to his face. "I don't care if you raise kangaroos. It simply doesn't matter anymore. It never should have mattered. When I saw sheep on the ranch last June, I saw red. I kept thinking about Granddad and how furious he would have been at Dad. Then, when Les told me whose sheep they were...."

Sloan turned his head and pressed his lips to the palm of her hand. "It's been quite a summer," he murmured.

"Yes." Maggie drew a weary breath. "Oh, Sloan, what am I going to do? I know Dad wants the ranch again."

She wasn't angry anymore; she'd talked anger out of her system. But she still didn't see the obvious solution. It was clear to Sloan, but he was hesitant about presenting it. It would be much better if Maggie reached it on her own, or, at least, reached the point where she would be receptive to hearing it from him.

He put his arms around her and brought her close to him. "We'll figure it out, Maggie. I promise you that." He felt her body heave with a sigh, and his lips moved on her hair.

"I should call them," she said.

Sloan heard the reluctance in her tone. "Would you like me to make the call and tell them you're all right?"

Maggie raised her head from his chest to see him. "You wouldn't mind? It's just that . . . well, I'm not quite ready to . . ."

"I understand." Sloan took her chin. "I love you." He waited, and he swore he saw love in her eyes. But he also saw confusion. "It's all right," he said softly, and kissed her.

He'd intended only a gentle, consoling kiss, but he felt her response and then couldn't tear his mouth from hers. Every kiss they shared was like that. Their physical reaction to one another was too strong to stay distanced from it.

In seconds they were straining to one another, needing more than a kiss. He felt her tongue enter his mouth, and the blood in his body leaped and surged to his groin. His hand went under her skirt and stroked the warm skin of her thighs, working its way up.

She unbuttoned his shirt and pushed her hands into it, caressing his chest, curling her fingers into the hair on it. Her mouth left his, only to feather against it, her breath heating his lips with sweet, hot moisture. "Do you want me?" she whispered raggedly.

"Lord, yes. Do you doubt it?"

"I need you."

He pressed her back into the couch, weighting her down with the intensity of his desire. "You'll have me. Let me make that call. I'll only be a minute." He slipped away from her and walked to the desk. Maggie heard the faint clicks of her telephone number being punched out.

"Hello, Sarah. I'm calling to tell you that Maggie is here with me.

"Yes, she's fine. We've been talking. She'll call you herself later." Maggie felt Sloan's eyes on her, then heard him say firmly, "In the morning, Sarah. She'll call you in the morning."

Maggie brought her gaze to him. He was beautifully rumpled, his shirt unbuttoned and gaping from his jeans, his hair mussed, his eyes heavy with sexual promises. She dampened her lips and smoothed back her hair, wondering how her parents would take her spending the night at Sloan's house.

She sighed. It didn't matter. They would know soon enough about Sloan and her.

"Yes, I'll tell her. Good night, Sarah."

He put the phone down and returned to the sofa. His eyes were dark blue and probing hers. "Your mother said to tell you that they love you," he said quietly.

She nodded slowly, not disputing it. Then she held her arms up. "I still need you," she whispered brokenly.

Sloan got up, took her hand and pulled her to her feet. Then he bent slightly and lifted her up into his arms. "I need you, too. Let's go to bed."

Twelve

———

Sloan's room was large and airy, with white walls and tasteful cherrywood furniture. Maggie barely noticed it. Her mind was sluggish, her thoughts disoriented and hazy. She was running on adrenaline, driven by chemistry. Sloan seemed like the only reality tonight and she felt obsessive in her need of him.

They undressed quickly in the light of the bedside lamp and fell into bed together. Their bare bodies tightly intertwined, arms and legs wound around each other. There, in Sloan's bed, in Sloan's arms, Maggie felt safe. Safe from what, she didn't know, but she had an almost mystical feeling that this was where she belonged.

For a few minutes she basked in the sensation. He was warm and solid and completely male. With him she felt her own gender more acutely. Only in his arms had she ever felt the true power of her femaleness. That's what he gave her, she suddenly realized, a sense of self and value.

Maggie's breath caught and she felt a rush of passion. Her hands roamed restlessly over Sloan's back and down to his firm, tight buttocks. "Make love to me," she whispered.

Sloan raised his head and saw the feverish need on her face. Even knowing it was rooted in the mauling her emotions had taken tonight, he couldn't resist the call, not when he loved her so much and her slightest touch set him on fire.

He thrust into her hard and fast, because that's what she wanted. Her cries of pleasure drove him deeper. It was wild and primitive, and maybe the most erotic sex he'd ever been a part of. He watched her face and saw when she was near the edge, and he drove her there, forcing her over the top.

Then she was weeping, and he withheld his own release to comfort and hold her. "I'm sorry, I'm sorry," she whispered, her voice thick with tears. "I used you...Sloan, I'm sorry."

"Don't. Hush. It's all right. I understand." He pressed kisses to her wet face. "If you can't turn to the man you love, who can you turn to?"

She sniffled and brushed at her eyes. "I do love you." Her voice cracked.

His heart seemed to take wing and soar. "I know you do, but tell me again."

"I love you, I really, honest-to-God love you. I tried not to. I tried so hard not to."

He smoothed the damp hair back from her forehead. Her face was flushed and moist and utterly beautiful. "I know you did."

"I didn't think there was room in my well-planned life for a man. Any man, Sloan. But you, especially."

"Because of my sheep."

"And Helen White." Maggie restlessly threw an arm to the pillow above her head, and Sloan saw that her emotions were still not completely at peace. "I did everything I could to keep you out of my life. I knew today that I'd lost the battle, but I still didn't want to admit it. Not really admit it.''

Their bodies were still united. He was keeping most of his weight off of her by supporting himself on his upper arms on either side of her, but he was becoming exceedingly aroused. He'd given her what she'd needed, denying his own need, but it was starting to get the better of him.

He moved just a little, withdrawing, then sliding back into her heat. Her eyes flashed to his. "You didn't . . . ?"

"No." He performed another slow slide.

They stared into each other's eyes. A bright light of excitement had ignited in Maggie's. "You're in my blood," she whispered huskily.

His voice was low, guttural, influenced by the depth of sexuality between them. "I hope so, sweetheart, because you're sure as hell in mine. I wanted to do this the first time I kissed you. Did you know that?"

He was moving slowly, long, delicious plunges that were glazing her eyes again. "I knew. It scared me. No one had ever kissed me like that before." Her voice had grown breathless. "I was very . . . inexperienced."

His eyes held hers. "I wasn't much different. But I knew I wanted you, from the first time I saw you."

"We were too young then for this kind of lovemaking."

The pupils of his eyes were pinpoints of desire. "This kind? What kind of lovemaking is this, Maggie?"

She took several labored breaths. Her lashes fluttered, her eyes darted. But the question burned her mind. She couldn't escape it, nor its implications. The options and choices and priorities she'd been struggling with flashed here and there in her brain, like lightning bugs. She tried to elude them all, but the disorder continued, and she looked at Sloan with bewildered eyes.

And then the strangest thrill of awareness zinged through her. She saw the love on his face, a blinding, glowing emotion. She saw hope and urgency and just a touch of despair.

She saw him as a person, as a flesh and blood man who wanted to weld their futures together. She saw him as the man she loved, the only man she had ever loved.

Something let go inside of her then, all the tension and strain she'd been living with. She felt soft, warm tears in her eyes, and her body was suddenly liquid with undisguised feelings. "It's love, isn't it?" she whispered. "Real love. The kind that lasts forever."

All movement stopped. Sloan stared down at her and saw something new and free in her eyes. His blood roared in his ears with real elation, not the pseudo, premature jubilation he'd felt before Maggie had arrived.

"Oh, Maggie, my sweet, sweet Maggie," he whispered, near tears, too. He kissed her lips with profound tenderness, again, then again. And when the excitement arose in them this time, it was accompanied by the euphoric headiness of naked and exposed feelings.

They were lying quietly. Sloan's left arm was beneath Maggie's pillow, his right across her waist. He'd turned off the lamp, and the only light in the room was reflected moonlight. Neither was sleeping, although they'd both planned to.

Maggie spoke, her voice a husky murmur in the darkness. "I shouldn't have asked them, Sloan."

"Asked who what, honey?"

"My folks. I never should have asked them to sell the ranch to me. I pointed out how the place was a financial drain the way it was, but that certainly couldn't have been news to them. Obviously they were handling it. If it had been too much, they would have put the ranch up for sale without my input."

"Makes sense." Sloan stirred, and his body molded closer to hers. Passion was sated, though, and he felt only contentment at their intimacy.

"On the other hand," Maggie mused. "Maybe they didn't want to sell to a stranger. Mother was upset that I offered to pay for something that would be mine someday, anyway. Maybe they always had intended to keep the place intact for me." She paused. "Sloan, do you think that's possible?"

"Entirely possible."

"I really do believe that they've always known what the place means to me."

"I'm sure they have."

Maggie was silent for a stretch, then said, "Sloan, I said some things tonight, about Mother and Dad not loving me. I don't really believe that."

"You were upset, honey. Believe me, I've already forgotten it."

"They're just . . . well, a little different. And they're so close to each other."

"For which you should be thankful."

"Yes, I should. And I am. So many of my friends' parents are divorced."

"Or dead, honey."

Maggie turned her face and kissed him. "I'm sorry," she whispered, knowing she'd just caused him some painful memories.

They settled back into a comfortable silence. It was getting late, but Sloan was more than willing to forego sleep until Maggie was ready. She was gradually approaching the conclusion he'd reached earlier, and he wouldn't have stopped her emotional expansion for anything in the world.

Then he heard the start of what he'd been waiting for. "I'm going to have to sell it back to them, aren't I?"

"Have to?" he questioned softly. "You don't *have* to do anything, Maggie."

"Oh, yes—" Maggie stopped the hasty rebuttal in midstream. "All right, maybe I phrased that wrong. I'm considering offering the ranch back to my folks." Then she bit her lip and buried her face in Sloan's chest. "Oh, it hurts," she whispered raggedly.

He stroked her hair. "I know," he soothed.

"I had such big plans."

"I know," he repeated softly.

"Les and I worked so hard. Everything is done except the barn and house, and then I was going to start on the fields. The Angus...the Thoroughbreds...even Bonnie and Clyde. Sloan, I wanted Bonnie and Clyde so much."

"You can have Bonnie and Clyde," he said quietly. "And the Thoroughbreds, too."

Maggie stiffened. "How?"

It was time to say his piece. Sloan pulled away from her, sat up and reached for the lamp switch. Maggie brushed the long, dark hair from her face and sat up, too, a puzzled look in her eyes. Absently, she brought the end of the sheet to her breasts, intent on the almost stern expression on Sloan's face. "What is it?" she asked. "What's wrong?"

"I said I wasn't ever going to mince words again with you, Maggie, and I've been doing that all evening. But you needed to sort things out. I think you did that, and did it very well, too. Now I've got something to say."

He seemed—angry? No, not angry. Resolute. Yes, that was the word, resolute. And slightly defensive, as if prepared to combat any reluctance on her part to listen. It surprised Maggie and made her rather uneasy. They'd attained such lovely closeness tonight, or so she'd felt, and it was unnerving to realize he might not have been in as much accord with her views as she'd thought.

"Please say it," she invited with a noticeable tremor in her voice.

He nodded solemnly. "I asked you to marry me today, and you talked about your ranch. I know what it means to you, so I didn't press the issue. I firmly believed we could and would eventually find a way to be together. To be married.

"Now there's a way. You didn't seek it, I didn't seek it, but we have it, all the same. You said you were wrong to push your folks into selling the ranch to you. I won't judge that, Maggie. Maybe you were, maybe you weren't. You're an intelligent, bright woman, and I feel strongly about one thing. Whatever you did, you thought it was right at the time."

"Yes," she whispered, deeply shaken by the tone in which Sloan was speaking.

"I'm offering you everything I am, everything I have. You can raise and breed your Thoroughbreds on this ranch. You can consult with the Labradors' owner and bring Bonnie and Clyde here. There's no room for the Angus, however. This is a sheep ranch, and that's the one thing I can't change for you. It's always been a sheep ranch, I've always been a sheepman, I probably always will. I think you've come to grips with that, though.

"But everything else, Maggie, this house, this land, me. It's all yours, if you want it. Your parents still need your place. They wouldn't be back if they didn't. They're still young, and maybe the new start you've given them is all the impetus they need to really take hold and make something of the place. Sell it back to them. Move in here, Maggie. Be my wife. Be my partner. I'd like a partner, a woman to work with me and build our ranch into the best there is, a woman who understands what land can mean to a man, a woman who melts when I touch her and who makes my knees weak with a smile. I need *you*, Maggie. I love you, and if you only love me half as much, we can't fail. Marry me, Maggie."

Tears were streaming down Maggie's cheeks. "You . . . you've stunned me," she whispered.

"I meant to."

His form was swimmingly indistinct through her tears. "I'm not sure of what to say."

He took a breath. "Where are your doubts? Where do they lie?"

She looked away from him, but saw little of the charming room.

"Maggie, I proposed this afternoon. This can't be a complete surprise."

"It's not. Or the proposal isn't. But the rest of it..." Her dark, wet eyes moved back to him. "Sloan, I would never say yes to a man just because he has a ranch to offer me."

He stared, then smiled. And finally he couldn't hold back the laughter bubbling up within him. "Maggie Holloway, believe me. No one who knows you would ever accuse you of marrying a man for his *sheep* ranch."

"No, I suppose not," she conceded. "But won't you wonder if I said yes because of having no ranch of my own, just the same?"

Sloan's heart began to knock against his ribs. "Did you say yes?"

She'd already said yes, in her soul. He'd moved her so much with that speech, she would have said yes if he'd told her they would be living in a city after the wedding. It was only added bliss to visualize the future he'd painted.

No, it wouldn't be on Holloway land. But she'd tried to rush a dream. She should have accepted what she knew so well, that Bert had always run back to the ranch after one of his schemes didn't pan out.

Maggie's love for Sloan swelled within her until she felt like bursting. She lowered the end of the sheet she'd been holding at her breasts, then moved to him and slid onto his lap. His arms went around her. She took his face in her hands. "I'm saying yes now," she said softly. "I love you more than I ever thought it was possible to love anyone."

"You'll never regret it," he said hoarsely, and their lips met in a warm exchange of love.

When Maggie could speak, she returned the ardent promise. "You'll never regret it, either, my love."

They snuggled down beneath the covers again, and Sloan snapped off the lamp. Curled together, they both closed their eyes.

"I'll call Dad and Mother first thing in the morning," Maggie murmured.

"Maybe we should just go over and talk to them. We've got a lot to tell them."

"Good idea. Yes, we'll do that." Sighing, Maggie nestled closer.

"I'm happy, Maggie, happier than I've ever been."

Happy? Maggie pondered the word. She'd thought her happiness laid with the ranch, possessing it, living on it.

The summer flicked through her mind, and with the thousand fleeting images, one stood out. Sloan. Then a door opened, and she caught a glimpse of the future. A lovely warm serenity washed over her, a sense of love and security and of life fulfilled.

"I'm happy, too," she said softly.

A minute later she realized that Sloan was sleeping and hadn't heard her. She smiled and closed her eyes. She would have years to tell him how happy he made her.

* * * * *

SILHOUETTE·INTIMATE·MOMENTS®

**Premiering in September,
a captivating new cover
for Silhouette's most adventurous
series!**

Every month, Silhouette Intimate Moments sweeps
you away with four dramatic love stories rich in
passion. Silhouette Intimate Moments presents
love at its most romantic, where life is exciting
and dreams do come true.

**Look for the new cover next month,
wherever you buy Silhouette® books.**

2IMNC-1

Silhouette Books®

Appearing in October
for a return engagement, Nora Roberts's
bestselling 1988 miniseries featuring

THE O'HURLEYS!
Nora Roberts

And making his debut in a brand-new title, a very special
leading man . . . Trace O'Hurley!

In 1988, Nora Roberts introduced THE O'HURLEYS!—a close-knit
family of entertainers whose early travels spanned the country. The
beautiful triplet sisters and their mysterious brother each experience
the triumphant joy and passion only true love can bring, in four books
you will remember long after the last pages are turned.

Don't miss this captivating miniseries in October—a special collec-
tor's edition available wherever paperbacks are sold.

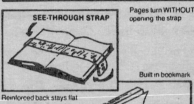